EMERALD GREEN

Laura Flanagan leaves Ireland to go to Australia and begin a new life there. During the flight to Australia she meets young horseman Declan Martin, taking the Irish champion Lancelot's Pride to race for the Melbourne Cup. But when Laura tells him she must find an Australian husband in order to live there, Declan doesn't handle it well and in Singapore they part bad friends. However when he walks into the Irish pub where she's working in Melbourne, the attraction is still there. Can Laura recognize true love before it's too late? Will Lancelot's Pride win the Melbourne Cup?

Books by Heather Graves
Published by The House of Ulverscroft:

FLYING COLOURS
RED FOR DANGER
STARSHINE BLUE

HEATHER GRAVES

EMERALD GREEN

Complete and Unabridged

ULVERSCROFT
Leicester

First published in Great Britain in 2008 by
Robert Hale Limited
London

First Large Print Edition
published 2009
by arrangement with
Robert Hale Limited
London

British Library CIP Data

Graves, Heather.
  Emerald green
  1. Irish- -Australia- -Fiction. 2. Horse racing- -
  Australia- -Melbourne (Vic.)- -Fiction.
  3. Love stories. 4. Large type books.
  I. Title
  823.9′2–dc22

  ISBN 978–1–84782–742–5

Published by
F. A. Thorpe (Publishing)
Anstey, Leicestershire

Set by Words & Graphics Ltd.
Anstey, Leicestershire
Printed and bound in Great Britain by
T. J. International Ltd., Padstow, Cornwall

This book is printed on acid-free paper

PROLOGUE

When Laura returned to Ireland after her extended trip to Australia, she found everything changed, even her mother. Before she left, they had been more like sisters than mother and daughter, as close as best friends. But now Bridie seemed jumpy and distant, distracted even, giving Laura the impression that she was keeping some great secret — probably a new man. Oh, she was used to her mother's flirting; she had been playing the merry widow for years. They had even laughed about her widening circle of men friends, taking none of them seriously. But this was different. She shrugged off her daughter's enquiries and would never say where she was going.

'This isn't like you, Mam.' Laura tackled her at last as she sat on her mother's bed, watching Bridie prepare for another night out on the town, applying a dark red lipstick that didn't suit her. Far from flattering Bridie's delicate colouring, it made her look older than her forty-seven years. In the past, Laura would have been able to say so without giving offence. Not now.

1

Laura sighed, trying again. 'What's happening to us, Mam? You used to tell me everything but right now you treat me as if I'm the enemy, shutting me out. What have I done?'

'You? Nothin', darlin'. Nothin' at all.' Bridie gave her a brittle smile.

'I think you're seeing someone. And it's getting serious.' She tried not to sound accusing. 'You are, aren't you?'

'So what if I am?' Bridie said defensively, turning to glare at her. 'I'm not all that old, you know. Not quite ready for slippers and a shawl.'

'Oh, Mam. I never said you were.'

'And you don't have to look so disapproving. Your father's been gone to his grave for more than ten years now an' I don't have to feel guilty for wantin' to see someone new.' She stuck her chin in the air, as if challenging Laura to say otherwise.

'Of course not. But who is this man? And how long have you known him?'

'If you must know, his name's Stanley Winton and he's an American. A very wealthy American,' she added with a mischievous smile.

'Oh!' Laura breathed a sigh of relief. 'Just a visitor, then?'

'I'll tell you all about him, I promise. But

not right now.' Bridie glanced at her watch. 'I'm runnin' late.'

Laura said no more, thinking there must be more to all this than her mother was telling and, for the first time in her life, she felt excluded from her mother's confidence and completely alone. Having been away from Ireland only a matter of months, she had returned home to find the world had shifted and moved on without her, alienating her from all that had been so dear and familiar before. She had nothing in common with the girls who had once been her friends. Taking up with new boyfriends, college courses or jobs, none of them wanted to hear Laura's tales of a country far away — a country they were never likely to visit. Who would have thought six months could make such a difference?

It wasn't long before she learned more about Stanley Winton. An American, tracing his Irish roots, he had turned up in the Dublin travel agency where her mother worked. Her mother was starry-eyed, saying how he had conducted an old-fashioned courtship, bombarding her with presents and flowers, sweeping her off her feet. With Laura away overseas, there had been no one to urge caution or put the brakes on this burgeoning romance, which had now developed into a raging love affair.

Finally came the night when her mother didn't come home at all, leaving only an indistinct message on the answering machine. Something about being sorry but she was too far away to get home.

Laura had tried to call Bridie at work the next day, only to be told she hadn't come in.

'Matter of fact, I was about to ring you.' Mr Sampson, the owner and manager of the travel agency, sounded very put out. 'We thought your mother must be sick. It's not like her to let us down.'

'No,' Laura said slowly. 'I'll contact you at once if I hear anything, Mr Sampson.'

'Yes,' he said briskly. 'Please do.'

Bridie didn't arrive back home until the evening of that same day and this time she had Stanley in tow.

'Mam, where have you been?' Laura greeted her at the door, on the verge of tears. 'Don't you know I've been worried sick about you?'

Bridie glanced at Stan and they giggled like conspirators. 'Will you listen to it?' she said to Stanley. 'Not even nineteen an' she's behavin' as if I'm the kid around here.'

Laura saw red. 'Well, you're behaving like one, Mam. How could you be so irresponsible? Mr Sampson was worried, too. He was very upset.'

4

'Sampson?' Her mother's smile faded. 'Lordy. He didn't ring here after me, did he?'

'No. I rang him because I didn't know where you were.'

'Well, great. You might at least have covered for me and said I was sick.'

'Bridie — Bridie, love.' Stanley caught her around the waist. Too familiarly, Laura thought. 'That ole job of yours don' matter none. You don' have to be nobody's gofer no more. We're gettin' hitched, remember? An' you're comin' home with me to Miami — '

'Miami?' Laura repeated, hoping she had misheard.

'Stanley, hush!' Bridie placed two fingers over his mouth to quiet him. 'All in good time. I have to square it with Laura first.'

'Square what?' Laura glowered at them, hands on hips. She didn't like the way this conversation was going. And she didn't like this Stanley either with his 'good ole boy' accent, standing there smirking at her. She didn't like him at all.

'Oh, darling. Don't look like that.' Bridie tried to hug her but Laura pulled away, dodging her embrace. 'Please try to understand. At my age you have to grab what happiness you can, before it's too late. Stanley has done me the honour of asking me to marry him — and I have accepted.'

5

'Accepted? Now just a moment, Mam, you need to slow down a bit. You've only known him a couple of months.' She glanced at Stan as if he were an unpleasant insect. 'He's a holiday-maker, for heaven's sake.'

'Darling, I know how it looks. I know it all seems a bit sudden. But it was love at first sight, wasn't it, Stan?' She squeezed the man's hand and he nodded, smiling at her indulgently. 'And you won't be left out. You'll be coming with us to Miami, won't she, Stan?'

'Wha — ' For just a moment the man's eyes widened in horror before he shrugged and mumbled, 'Yeah. I s'pose. If that's what you want.'

'It's not as if we have anything to stay here for.' Bridie was gabbling now. 'You're finished with school now and we have no ties. It's only a question of giving up the flat — '

'Mam, please. Let me say something first.' Laura held up a hand to stem the flow of words. 'If you really want to get married and go to America, that's fine with me. I'm happy for you. But please don't expect me to join you.'

'Ah well, that's fine with us, too,' Stanley said, brightening at once until Bridie hushed him again.

'Why ever not?' she said.

Laura shrugged. 'I'd rather not say. I just don't want to, that's all.'

'Well, we can't always do as we want, Laura.'

'Why not? You are.'

'That's right. But you're still only eighteen years of age and while you might consider yourself all grown up, I'm here to tell you you're not.' Bridie waved a hand at their sparsely decorated flat. 'You can't afford to live here on your own. Even with that job at the pub, you can't make enough to pay rent, even if you get someone to share. But if you come to America with us, you can finish your education, maybe even go on to university and — '

'Mam, we've been through all this before I went to Australia. I have no interest in going to uni just for the sake of it. I can't be a doctor; I faint at the sight of blood. I hate lawyers and I don't want to teach — I can't think of anything worse.'

'But you'll never amount to anything, pulling beer in a pub,' Bridie wailed, wringing her hands.

'I might.' Laura tried to lighten the mood. 'Some film director might come in and discover me. I'll be his new Irish sensation — '

'Ah, don't be silly. Things like that don't

happen in real life. No. If you don't want to come to America with us, I'll have to ask Auntie Kit if you can move in with her.'

'Please don't. I can't think of anything worse — except maybe going to America with you an' Stan — '

'There's no need to be rude.'

'I know but that's how I feel. An' I won't be pushed into bein' an unpaid servant for your old Auntie Kit. She'd have me runnin' up an' down those stairs a hundred times a day. An' her house is horrible too — she keeps all the windows shut an' it smells of boiled cabbage an' old knickers.'

Stan started to laugh until he saw Bridie wasn't amused and turned it into a cough.

'Then what are you going to do?' Bridie glared at her daughter. 'There's nobody else.'

'Oh yes there is.' Smitten by a wonderful idea, Laura smiled for the first time. 'I can go back to Australia. Daniel said I'd be welcome any time.'

'Maybe he did. But he won't be expectin' you back so soon. An' didn't he just get married?'

'To Foxie, yes. I told you — I was their bridesmaid. They have loads of money, a racing stables and two massive houses. I could live there for ever without getting in their way.'

Bridie still looked unsure. 'Yes but what about work?'

Laura considered this for a moment, thinking it best not to mention the need for a work permit and the difficulty of obtaining one. 'Oh, I'm an experienced bartender now,' she said airily. 'I can always get casual work in a pub.'

And Bridie, who heard what she wanted to hear because she was in love, gave in, allowing Laura to do as she wished. Her daughter was to fly out from Heathrow on the same day as she went to America with her Stanley. And a bemused Stanley, while not exactly thrilled to be asked to stump up for a one-way ticket to Melbourne, decided it was cheap at the price to be rid of Bridie's recalcitrant daughter. She seemed far too perceptive of his faults and made him nervous, tweaking his toupée. So far as he was concerned, the more miles that separated them, the better he would like it.

When the moment of parting finally came, mother and daughter clung together, weeping noisily. They realized, for perhaps the first time, that they were heading to opposite ends of the earth and had no idea when they would see one another again. Glancing round to see who was noticing this unseemly display of emotion, Stanley shifted from one foot to the other, anxious to be gone. Hearing once more the final call for Laura's flight to Melbourne, they broke free, both wiping tears away with inadequate tissues. Without a backward glance, Laura picked up her bag and ran for the doors which separated those who would travel from those who must stay behind.

⋆ ⋆ ⋆

'Declan! Are you here, lad?' John O'Shea, the stable foreman, peered into the gloom at the back of the stables, calling for his young assistant as he shook himself like a dog to remove the worst of the rain from his coat. In this part of Ireland, it wasn't uncommon for it to rain without stopping for fifty of the fifty-two weeks of the year. 'Ah, there you are!' he exclaimed as Declan emerged from the small, overcrowded office to see what he wanted. 'Great news! The boss has finally decided. He wants to send Lancelot's Pride to the Melbourne Spring Racing Carnival — hopefully to try for the Melbourne Cup.'

Declan nodded, unsmiling. He didn't share the optimism of his uncle, who owned this successful, high-profile racing stables. So far as he was concerned, it was a rare horse that could travel 12,000 miles, race in altered climatic conditions on cruel tracks with no give in them and come home a winner. He knew of several thoroughbreds who had gone out with high hopes only to be buried there. And Lancelot's Pride was his particular favourite, his pet; he didn't want to see him broken on the wheel of his uncle's ambition.

'Oh? And when did he reach this momentous decision? Just putting Lance on a plane and getting him there is no guarantee of acceptance into any of their major events.'

'Don't be so negative. He won well enough for us at Ascot, didn't he?'

'Yeah. On soft ground after overnight rain. Melbourne's going to be very different. They've been suffering drought conditions in that part of Australia.'

'And I've seen the Melbourne Cup run in such rain storms, the jockeys have come home covered in mud.'

Declan shrugged, still unhappy. 'I'll talk to Uncle Tavis about it tonight.'

'Well, try not to upset him. This is the first time I've seen him smiling in more than a month and we all know the stables could do with a boost. The owners expect it. We haven't had a significant win overseas since Holiday Girl went to France.'

Although he was longing to go straight to his uncle, setting his doubts before him at once, Declan could see the sense in allowing him to enjoy and finish his evening meal before raising the subject of Lancelot's Pride. Tavis Martin could be unpredictable and difficult to deal with at the best of times, his prideful, half-Spanish ancestry making him volatile. Declan knew little about the past except that the two Martin brothers had married two sisters in a double wedding. He could remember little of his early years except they had all seemed to be happy, with everyone getting along. Until his parents had died together in a freak accident on a railway crossing.

Tavis had taken the boy into his household when he was just five years old. A busy man whose own marriage was childless, Tavis didn't welcome this turn of events, leaving it to Maureen, his wife, to provide the love and support the child needed. It wasn't until Declan grew old enough to be useful and ride track work for him that Tavis began to take an interest in the nephew his wife had always adored.

'We're so lucky, Tavis,' she would tell him, trying to get him to take an interest in the lad. 'He's healthy and happy. Who could wish for a better son?'

'Hmmph,' Tavis would say, scowling, always searching for some criticism to bring the boy down. 'He'll never amount to anything, though. Hopeless at school.'

'That's not his fault.' Maureen was quick to defend him. 'The teachers said he may be dyslexic.'

'Dyslexic. Sounds like a fancy word for laziness, if you ask me.'

'Well, I'm not asking you.' Annoyed by his dismissive attitude, for once Maureen stood up to her husband. 'And if you'd come to the school with me when they asked to see us about it, you'd know. It's a common condition and doesn't mean that he's lazy or stupid. His brain perceives things differently, that's all.'

'Don't care what you say. It still sounds like a bunch of excuses to me.'

★　★　★

But now Declan was twenty-six years old and his uncle had to acknowledge his worth to the stables. He knew that Tavis would listen to his opinion and hear him out, even if he didn't act upon his suggestions right away. He helped his aunt to clear away the main course and serve cheese and biscuits followed by coffee, before daring to raise the subject of Lancelot's Pride. Maureen hesitated, looking as if she would like to give him advice on how to handle the matter but, with Tavis sitting

13

staring at them, it was impossible. Instead, she gave a small sigh, picked up her coffee and said there was something she wanted to watch on TV.

Declan stood up as if he were about to leave also and then placed his hands on the back of the kitchen chair. If this talk with his uncle should degenerate into an argument, he preferred to do it standing up. He asked his question without preamble, knowing the man's attention span would be short.

'Johnno tells me you're thinking of sending Lance to Melbourne to have a crack at the Cup?'

'We're not thinking about it — we're doing it.' Tavis played with the crumbs on his plate without meeting his nephew's gaze. 'The flight is booked. The vet has gone over the horse and is preparing the necessary certificates. Everything is in place and already arranged.'

'But how can it be while Conor is still in Hong Kong?' Declan was thinking of their travelling foreman, who had already been overseas for several months. 'And I know he's hoping to take a break and spend some time with the family when he comes back.'

'Conor is leaving us. His choice.' Tavis looked up at him then. 'If he prefers to put his personal life before the good of the stables — ' He shrugged one shoulder.

'But you can't force him into a choice like that! It's not fair. He's been with us for years.'

'I don't need you to tell me what's fair. As I said, it's his own decision. He's taking up a more lucrative offer elsewhere.'

Declan was silent for a moment, digesting this news. 'So who's travelling to Australia with Lance? You'll need someone who knows the horse and you'll be hard pressed to find someone as reliable as Conor.'

Tavis laughed shortly. 'Who better than family? I'm promoting you, Declan. You're old enough to take the responsibility now. You shall be our new travelling foreman.'

'Me?' Declan had to prevent himself from staring at his uncle, slack-jawed. 'But I don't have the experience. If you expected me to do this, you should have let me go out with Conor as his assistant before. I need to learn the ropes.'

'What's to learn? You already know all there is to know about horses. Anything else you'll pick up as you go along.'

Declan was still regarding him, shaking his head.

Tavis scowled. 'I hope you're not going to be foolish enough to look a gift horse in the mouth? Your first assignment will be to take Lancelot's Pride to Australia for me. After all, it's not as if you have any ties here. Not now Lucy's married to someone else.'

The young man almost flinched. Only someone as insensitive as his uncle would remind him of that. The loss of his childhood sweetheart was still a raw wound. They had been the most striking couple during their last year at school — the fair, almost ethereal Lucy a perfect foil for Declan, with his dark eyes and swarthy good looks, inherited from more than one Spanish ancestor.

'Declan, we take each other too much for granted,' she had said. 'We've been jogging along together for years now and you've never once hinted at marriage — not even an engagement.'

'I'll get around to it, Luce. Early days yet.'

'But it isn't. I shall be twenty-six next year.'

'That's not old.'

'I know. But I want to be married, Declan. And have lots of children before it's too late.'

'People can't afford such big families these days.'

'People with big families never could. But that's what I want from life. So does Jonas.'

'Jonas, is it? Sounds like a biblical prophet. Has he got a beard and long toenails?'

'Don't be nasty, Declan. You never pay me compliments or say I look nice and you don't even bother to say you love me any more. But

Jonas does — all the time. He appreciates me and — and he's exciting — '

'Meaning I'm not, I suppose?'

'You could be — if you wanted to be.' For just a moment Lucy hesitated, sounding wistful and looking as if she might relent. Instead she gave herself a little shake and stiffened her resolve. 'But Jonas is a romantic. He makes me feel special — that I'm the most wonderful girl in the world.'

'Infatuation,' he muttered.

'What if it is? At least that's better than plain old indifference. You and I have been rubbing along like a pair of old slippers.'

'I'm not indifferent to you, Lucy.' He felt a sense of rising panic, realizing at last he was losing her. 'Sure'n you know that?'

'It's too late, Declan. It doesn't matter any more. I'm not here to twist your arm or get you to make promises you're not ready to keep. And you're not going to talk me out of it. I'm marrying Jonas next month.'

And she had. Leaving Declan with a gaping hole in his life. If he were honest with himself, he had indeed taken Lucy for granted and if she'd been the love of his life, they would have been married by now. But he missed her in his bed and had been surprised to feel so bereft.

And only now, with Tavis's implacable gaze

upon him as he waited for a response, did he begin to understand his uncle's true feelings towards him. Far from being indifferent to the child who had been foisted upon him some twenty odd years ago, he might actively dislike him. Why else would he send him on this globe-trotting commission which would keep him almost permanently away from home? The older he grew, the more he resembled his father — Maureen kept saying so. And there was often rivalry between brothers. Had Tavis secretly detested Declan's father, too? This was a question better not asked.

But the more Declan considered the offer, the more he warmed to the idea. Why remain here in his uncle's house, when the only person to miss him would be his Aunt Maureen? She had taken the place of the mother he scarcely remembered, giving him all the love his uncle withheld. And yes, he would miss her, too, but he could call her each week and catch up — she would like that.

'Thank you, Uncle Tavis, for your faith in me,' he said at last. 'I will do my best to live up to it.'

'Good.' His uncle nodded, not even offering his hand to close the deal. 'You can take Wes as your strapper and track rider.'

18

'No. I'd rather take Jodie — Lance's regular strapper.'

His uncle scowled. 'Johnno won't like it. Jodie's his best girl.'

'And Lance is your best horse. It's a long journey and going to be hard on all of us. Lance will settle better with his own strapper. How soon do you want us to leave?'

'The Carnival doesn't start till the end of October. September should be soon enough.'

'And have Lance arrive jet-lagged and losing weight? It's July already. I'd rather leave as soon as possible to get him acclimatized.'

His uncle's scowl deepened. 'Those quarantine stables are expensive — I don't like it.'

'The whole exercise is expensive and it's rare for European horses to do very well there. We always underestimate the local talent.'

'So what are you trying to say?'

'Either afford to do the thing properly or forget it. If Lance goes to Australia, we must give him the best possible chance.'

For the first time Tavis sat back and smiled, appreciating that his nephew was standing up to him. 'Well, well,' he said, almost to himself. 'Give a lad a bit of authority and he can surprise you.'

'Yes and there's one more thing, Nunc.'

Declan used the nickname he knew Tavis hated. 'If this is indeed a promotion for me, I hope it's going to be reflected in my wages?'

Seeing his uncle's eyes widen and his face begin to turn an unhealthy red, Declan decided it was a good time to leave. It was only later that he remembered it had been his original intention to talk his uncle out of sending Lance to Melbourne at all. Too late now.

1

Unlike many people, Laura always enjoyed flying, even in Economy. Entirely as she expected, her new stepfather had turned mean, refusing to pay for her to travel in Business Class. Wealthy men didn't keep their money by being too generous.

At the same time, Bridie was querying Stanley's decision as they boarded their own flight to New York and a smiling stewardess was settling them into their comfortable seats in Business Class.

'Young people don't need pampering,' he assured her, patting her knee. 'They don' appreciate this kinda luxury an' their bones are young enough not to need it. Why? Did Laura fly Business Class the last time she went to Australia?'

'No, of course not but — '

'Face it, Bridie — she's goin' her own ways without us. Ain't that the truth?'

'Yes, but it would have been a nice gesture — a parting gift.'

Stanley grunted. He could see no point in heaping luxuries on an ungrateful stepdaughter, particularly when there was no one around to applaud and praise his generosity. 'She chose not to be part of our family.' He'd been repeating this like a mantra until it was starting to get on Bridie's nerves. 'As I recall, she said she could think of nothing worse.'

Bridie's frown only deepened so Stanley smiled widely and clapped his hands to show her the subject was closed. 'Now let me tell you all about my family, so you'll know who they are when you meet them. The parents are long gone, of course, but there's my younger brother, Cal, he's the brains of the family — an attorney in New York. I jus' know you'll love him and his wife, Essie. Then, when we travel down to Miami, you'll meet my sister, Fleur, and Aunt Cassie . . . '

Bridie sighed, trying to pay attention although she felt herself drifting off to sleep as Stanley droned on about the various members of his family. Cautiously, she lay back, taking care not to crush her new hairdo or crease her new suit. Before leaving London, she had treated herself to a well-cut designer model that flattered her slim figure together with a giant handbag made of the softest leather in a shade of butter yellow. The bag alone had cost more than she used to earn in a year but she didn't want to appear before Stanley's relatives looking provincial.

★　★　★

Laura, whose flight had been delayed for some late arrivals, was unconcerned, happy just to be going back to Australia. Foxie had seemed surprised when she phoned to say she was returning so soon but Daniel had been genuinely pleased. With little money and only a one-way ticket, she was well aware that if she hadn't been able to say she was staying with relatives, Australian Customs might not allow her into the country. Stanley's generosity had not extended to the provision of pocket money but she didn't care. There was something about the man that she didn't like and she didn't want to take any more from him than was absolutely necessary. It was bad enough being beholden to him for her plane ticket.

Economy was busy, as usual, and with few places to spare, but she was pleased to discover she had been allotted a window seat. Now, all she had to worry about was who might occupy the seats next to her on the non-stop flight to Singapore. She held her breath, catching sight of an enormous man in a business suit, sweating and struggling down the aisle towards her. She almost sighed with relief when he staggered past and laid claim to a seat several rows behind her. She

23

assessed each person who approached, expecting someone to occupy the vacant seats, but for a long time this didn't happen.

Finally, a dark-haired, energetic young man rushed down the aisle, threw his bag into the overhead locker, together with his suede jacket and slumped into the seat beside her, blowing out a long breath and closing his eyes.

She took stock of him, noticing that he was unusually pale; probably one of those people who didn't like flying. He seemed to be in his mid-twenties, tall but slender and wearing good quality jeans with a checked shirt. Unlike most of the other travellers, he had no briefcase nestling beside him. Not a man of business then. He had strong features with high cheekbones, his hair being thick, curly and even darker than her own, his eyelashes impossibly long. Why did girls never get eyelashes like those? She sighed, deciding that he probably came from some Mediterranean country — Spain, Italy, Greece or even the South of France. Languages were not her strong point and small talk would be impossible unless his English was good.

Sensing the intensity of her gaze, he opened his eyes and smiled, looking slightly surprised. Embarrassed to be caught staring at him, she gave him a shy smile in return and looked away to search for the airline magazine in the pocket on the back of the seat in front of her. Still aware of his scrutiny, she found the magazine and started to flick through it, hoping to find something to catch her interest and willing herself not to blush.

The light was flashing, warning passengers to fasten their seat belts, and the plane began its slow movement away from the terminal to take up its position, ready for take-off. No one had come to occupy the vacant seat on the aisle.

Then came the moment she found most exciting as the engines roared in unison, preparing to lift the big passenger jet off the ground At last they were on their way. Now the adventure could really begin. Closing his eyes once again, her fellow passenger let out a low groan and she saw he was gripping the arms of his seat so tightly, his knuckles were showing white. The plane rose into the air and banked, giving her a temporary view of the sprawl of the city below until it climbed even higher and clouds quickly obscured the view.

'It's OK.' She spoke to the man sitting next to her, whose eyes were still firmly closed. 'We're safely upstairs now. I don't think we're going to crash.'

He gave her a wry smile and nodded. 'I

know,' he said. 'I know I'm an eejit but I just hate take-off and landing. I can't help meself.'

'But you're Irish!' She gave a delighted laugh. 'An' here I was thinkin' you'd be Spanish or something and we wouldn't be able to talk.'

'Declan Martin.' He introduced himself, offering his hand. 'And you are?'

'Laura Flanagan.' His grip was warm and comforting and she continued to shake his hand vigorously, not really wanting to let go. And now he had stopped being pale and nervous, he really did have a lovely smile.

'Flanagan, eh? Well, it doesn't get more Irish than that. And you're right about my Spanish ancestry. As the story goes, we Martins are descended from a Spanish sailor washed ashore many years ago at the time of the Armada. An' then my grandmother went to Spain as a girl an' married a Catalan from Barcelona. He came back to Ireland with her an' spent the rest of his life complainin' about the weather.'

'We don't have anything half so interesting in our background.' Laura wrinkled her nose. 'Nothing but Irish, through all the generations. But I do have an Australian cousin. He lives in Melbourne and I'm on my way to see him now.'

'So you're travellin' right through to

Melbourne? That's great. So am I.' Declan smiled again, showing perfect teeth 'By the time we get there, we should be old friends.'

She smiled back at him, liking the idea. They chatted for a while, talking of places in Ireland familiar to both of them as they ate a very standard, mostly pre-packaged airline meal.

'It's the only thing I don't like about flying — the food.' Laura sighed, leaving most of it and pushing the tray away. 'You think you're starving an' then when it comes, you don't really want it at all. My mother is on her way to Miami with her new husband even as we speak — Business Class, of course.'

'Well, I'm glad they didn't send you Business Class,' Declan said, 'or we wouldn't have met.' Rather to his surprise, he found he was pleased to be sharing the flight with this friendly, ingenuous girl with those incredible, dark blue eyes. Eyes so dark that at first glance he had thought they were brown but, on looking more closely, he could see they were a startling cornflower blue. She seemed to have no qualms about saying exactly what came into her mind. He hadn't felt this at ease with a girl since losing Lucy and it cheered him to think he might at last be on the road to recovery. Since there was plenty of time, and he was a good listener, Laura told him all about her mother's new husband and her misgivings about him.

'I think he's creepy and insincere but she doesn't see it.' She gave a small shiver of distaste. 'He's dazzling her with the promise of luxury. In some ways my mam is a total innocent. She knows nothing at all about men.'

'And you do?' Declan said softly, suppressing a smile. It was hard to think of anyone more innocent or naïve than Laura. But then he found himself opening up to her, talking of things he'd never discussed with anyone, not even Lucy: his relationship with the uncle and aunt who adopted him and, finally, his promotion and the purpose of his visit to Australia.

'You're a horseman — of course. I should've guessed,' she said, wide-eyed. 'But surely your horse isn't travelling with us? On this plane?'

'Oh, no.' He laughed, reassuring her. 'He went on an earlier flight with Jodie, his strapper. Lance has special accommodation in cargo along with cabin crew specially trained to take care of horses.'

'So why aren't you travelling with them?'

'And let Jodie see me freak out on take-off and landing? I'd never hear the end of it.'

'But if you're a travelling foreman and she's

the strapper, she's bound to find out sooner or later. An' if she's your girlfriend, surely she'd want to help you?'

'Jodie isn't my girlfriend. She's completely devoted to horses.' Declan gave a bark of laughter, thinking of the snubnosed girl with frizzy red hair and a face full of freckles, swaggering about the stables in dirty jeans like a boy. Then he sobered, remembering how she had blushed and looked up at him through her eyelashes when he told her he had asked for her to be part of his team taking Lance to Australia, rather than the more experienced Wes. He would have to tread carefully there, making sure she wasn't getting the wrong idea.

'But what a coincidence!' Laura was almost bouncing in her seat. 'My cousin Daniel trains horses too — among other things. He and his wife have a racing stables in the country outside of Melbourne. We're sure to run into each other at one of the tracks while you're there.'

'That's right,' he agreed, 'but we could be rivals, too, if he has a runner in the Melbourne Cup?'

'Oh, I don't think so.' Laura looked less than assured. 'He has some good horses but I don't think he has any long-distance stayers like that.'

'I'm not sure my uncle's doing the right thing sending Lancelot's Pride to Melbourne. It's tough enough to have to travel so far without running a gruelling race at the end of it. I'll just hate it if anything happens to him.'

'Well, if it's any comfort to you, the veterinary people and stewards do everything in their power to make sure a horse is fit to run in that race. It's their showcase to the world and no one wants any accidents.'

Later, although the plane was travelling into constant daylight, the cabin staff closed the shutters over the windows and brought pillows to those who needed them. After the tensions of the day and the realization that the mother she had so loved might be lost to her for ever, Laura felt tears of self-pity pricking her eyes, so she turned away, pretending to compose herself for sleep. Soon the pretence became real and she fell into a deep and exhausted sleep lasting several hours. She awoke suddenly, with a snort, to discover that she had been resting her head on Declan's shoulder.

'I'm so sorry,' she murmured. 'I fell asleep on you. Did I snore?'

'Oh, yes.' He grinned at her. 'But no more than anyone else.'

'You're supposed to say, 'No, of course not — you were just breathing deeply.''

'Am I?' He shrugged. 'OK. I'll remember next time.'

'I'll try to see that there isn't a next time.'

Soon the pilot informed them that they were making good time and could expect to be landing in Singapore in just over an hour. Although they had left London around 11 a.m. and had been travelling for approximately twelve hours, they would arrive there at 7 a.m. local time.

'I fell in love with Australia the last time I went there.' Laura started a new conversation. 'The people are friendly and mostly the weather is great. I'm sure you'll love it, too.'

'And what do you plan to do when you get there?' Declan said by way of continuing their earlier conversation. He realized he had held nothing back of his own personal life, except for the trauma of losing Lucy. He wasn't ready to hear anyone's views on that. 'Do you have a job lined up?'

She shook her head. 'Doesn't matter, though. I'm sure I'll get temporary work — something to fill in until I get married.'

'Married?' Suddenly, he felt as if someone had kicked him in the stomach — hard. But he recovered quickly. What a fool he had been to start building a fantasy around this girl. Just because she smelled good and he'd liked the feel of her head on his shoulder. 'I don't think you mentioned you were engaged?'

'Well, no, I'm not,' she said, wishing she hadn't let her tongue run away with her. 'Not yet, anyway. But I will have to think about it seriously. If I want to remain in Australia permanently — as I do — I need to find an Australian husband. Because if I don't, they'll send me back to Ireland when my visa runs out.'

For a moment Declan stared at her before finding his voice. 'Laura, you have to be joking? I hope you are. Surely you don't have to go to such lengths. Didn't you say you have family there? Couldn't they sponsor you?'

Laura shrugged. 'I suppose so but it takes so long and I might still be sent back to Ireland to wait. No. Marriage is a better solution. It can't be all that difficult to fall in love.' Declan was still staring at her, unsmiling, and she found herself gabbling. 'And they just love the Irish accent. I'm sure there's heaps of Australian men who'd love to marry a nice Irish girl.' And she giggled nervously, trying to lighten the mood.

'To be frank, Laura, I'm surprised you can be so shallow.'

'Oh no, you don't understand, I — '

'I don't know when I heard of anything so

calculating, so — so cheap in the whole of my life.'

'Cheap?'

'Yes, cheap. Although I suppose you'll be selling yourself to the highest bidder.' He was working himself into a temper now. 'And how about this unsuspecting Australian? Does he have to be rich as well?'

'I don't know. I haven't thought about it.'

'Then maybe it's time you did. And how are you going to set about this entrapment? Via the internet? Or in the time-honoured way of getting yourself pregnant?'

'That's a horrible thing to say,' she said in a fierce whisper, glancing around. 'And keep your voice down. People are looking at you.'

'Let them.' He glared at their fellow passengers across the aisle, who had been watching their argument with increasing interest. They looked quickly away.

'And, anyway, what's it to you?' Laura persisted. 'You don't really know me. You didn't even know I existed twenty-four hours ago.'

He took a deep breath, controlling his irritation. 'You're right, of course. I don't. And it's absolutely no business of mine. I'm surprised, that's all. I took you for someone with higher principles.'

'Well, I'm sorry. But I can't afford them.'

Suddenly, tears pricked her eyes. Impatiently, she rubbed them away. Until yesterday, Bridie had always been there to advise and guide her, tell her where she was going wrong. But not any more. And now she was losing her new best friend. A lump of misery seemed to be blocking her throat as the tears threatened yet again. 'I still don't see why it makes you so angry, Declan,' she said in a small voice.

'It doesn't. Like I said, it's no business of mine.'

Still she felt bound to justify what she was saying. 'Sure'n isn't it the dream of most girls to get married and start a family? I'm jus' being practical — more up front and honest about it, that's all.'

'Practical!' he echoed, closing his eyes. Now she was starting to sound like Lucy. 'Let's drop it, shall we? We'll be landing in half an hour.'

She wanted to remind him that he'd promised her coffee while they waited for the ongoing flight to Melbourne but he was distant now, his expression closed, unapproachable. It didn't help to know it was all her own fault; she should have kept her plans to herself. After all, they were still only daydreams but it was too late to say so now. She didn't know how to reach him, to bring him back to the friendly, casual relationship they had shared before.

He said nothing more, becoming stiff and tense again as the plane lost height, preparing to land. He kept his eyes closed as it did so without incident and began rolling towards the terminal. When it finally stopped, the signs went off and the music started, everyone came to life and stood up, grabbing luggage from overhead lockers, anxious to leave the confined space. Declan reached for his coat, took out his bag and handed down hers.

'Goodbye, Laura,' he said. 'I hope you find what you're looking for. But remember, as the saying goes, there's no place like home.'

'That's just it,' she said in a small voice. 'I can't go back because there's no one there for me any more. Ireland is no longer my home.'

Suddenly, she looked so sad and alone that he relented. And, on impulse, before she realized what he would do, he leaned down and gave her a brief but far from tentative kiss on the lips. Her breath was sweet and tasted of incipient tears. 'Be careful, that's all.'

'Declan!' she murmured, wondering why she felt so disturbed by that kiss, irrationally longing for more. She pressed her fingers to lips that still tingled after he pulled away. But she could say nothing further because he was gone, striding down the length of the plane towards the exit, his mind already on other things. She sat back in her own seat, watching him leave, willing him to turn and wave at her one last time. But he disappeared without looking back at all.

'Is there a problem?' A young stewardess stopped to speak to her, noticing her unhappy expression. 'Anything I can do?'

'No, no, it's nothing.' Laura forced a smile, picked up her bag and hurried off the plane.

Over three hours were to pass before she could resume her flight to Melbourne. For part of the time, she looked in the duty-free shops, choosing presents for Daniel and Foxie. For Daniel she bought a bottle of the single malt whisky she knew he loved and for Foxie a bottle of Ivoire de Balmain. She didn't know what perfume Foxie liked but she was following the oldest present-giving rule — when in doubt, give something you'd like yourself.

Wandering through the shops took just over an hour and with time to spare before joining her fellow passengers in the departure lounge, she decided to look for Declan. After all, he had kissed her, even if he had been abominably rude. She wanted to find him, make peace and hold him to his promise of buying her coffee. But he was nowhere to be found.

She bought coffee for herself, realizing she didn't really want it, and then went to look for something to read. She chose a book, hoping it would make her laugh aloud as the blurb promised. It didn't. In fact, she found the unsubtle humour depressing and left it behind in the lounge when her flight was called. As she queued to board the plane, she kept looking for Declan, hoping he might turn up at the last minute, but she didn't see him there. At last, carried by the momentum of the other passengers, she found herself hurrying down the corridor towards the plane.

Once again, she had been given a window seat but this time the seat beside her was occupied by a large and excitable English lady, smelling of baby talc.

'Do you have relatives in Australia?' she said, continuing without waiting for Laura's reply. 'I do. It's always nice to see a friendly face at the end of a long journey.'

Without any input from Laura, she kept up a constant stream of chatter as she consumed large quantities of white wine. At last she fell asleep, sprawled in her seat and mouth agape; it wasn't a pretty sight. She didn't even wake when Laura squeezed past to go to the toilet and stretch her legs.

Deliberately, she walked down one aisle and then up the other, expecting to catch sight of Declan among the other passengers but he wasn't there. On the way back to her own seat, she ran into an older stewardess and decided to ask.

'Excuse me but I thought this was the connecting flight for passengers from Heathrow?' she said. 'On the first leg of our journey there was another passenger sitting beside me. I was expecting to see him again on this flight.'

The woman smiled gently. 'We have several flights out of Singapore, going to both Melbourne and Sydney. If your fellow traveller had been willing to go via Sydney, he might easily have changed to an earlier flight.'

'I see.' Laura gave her a wan smile, realizing she had let her tongue run away with her as usual; she shouldn't have been so open, telling Declan of her plans. Now, in spite of that kiss, it seemed he despised her enough to avoid her entirely by taking an earlier flight. She touched her finger to her lips again, remembering it.

'I do hope' — the woman was looking at her with almost motherly concern — 'that you didn't join the mile high club?'

'The what?' Laura had the feeling that this was a euphemism for something not to be applauded. 'Sorry. I don't know what you're talking about.'

'Sometimes, on long flights when people are travelling alone, they make friends too easily. It can result in a first date or even a one-night stand.'

Laura felt herself blushing furiously. 'But this is a public place,' she whispered, glancing around. 'How could they possibly? You can't be suggesting that people make love in the toilets?'

'When you've been flying as long as I have, there are no surprises.' The woman gave her a knowing smile.

Too embarrassed to continue the conversation, Laura turned and stumbled back to her seat to find her fellow passenger awake and awaiting their next meal.

'There you are, dear!' She peered at Laura and then recoiled. 'Not sick, are you? You were gone a long time and you do look a bit flushed. I hope you're not coming down with something contagious?'

'No,' Laura said through gritted teeth. 'I'm fine.'

★ ★ ★

On arrival in Melbourne, Laura held her breath as she fronted up to the Customs officer who examined her passport, hoping to impress him with a confident smile. He ignored it.

'You seem rather fond of us, miss.' He took note of her visas. 'Here not so long ago. What's the purpose of your journey this time? You do seem to have rather a lot of luggage.' He nodded towards the trolley containing her bags.

'I have relatives in Melbourne. I'll be staying with them.'

'I see.' He looked at her, raising his eyebrows. 'And do you have a return ticket?'

'Not yet,' Laura said, uncomfortable under his scrutiny. 'I'm not quite sure when I'm going to leave.'

Before stamping her passport and letting her go, he took note of her details and asked for a contact address in Melbourne. 'And make arrangements to leave before your visa expires,' He said, giving her a last, considering glance.

It was a relief to break free of the Customs area and enter the main terminal. As she had hoped but not really expected, her cousin was waiting for her and she leaped into his arms, flinging herself into his embrace.

'Oh, Daniel, it's so good to see you again.'

'Good to see you, too.' He grinned. 'Can I put you down now?'

'Oh sorry, sorry. Am I ruining your suit?' She got down and started patting imaginary dust off it. 'You're always so well turned out.'

'Laura, stop it. It's OK.' He caught sight of her trolley. 'Hey, that's rather a lot of luggage.'

'All my worldly goods,' she whispered.

'That so? I have the feeling you've got a lot to tell me, young lady.'

'Yes, I have. But first I want to hear about you. Is Foxie OK? And how's married bliss?'

His expression clouded. 'In what order do you want me to answer those questions?'

'I don't care. I just want you to tell me that everything's OK?'

'Later,' he said. By now they were at the car. He filled the boot with her smaller bags and wriggled the big one onto the back seat behind them. 'I'll bet you had to pay excess for this lot.'

'No but my new stepfather did.'

'Now why do I get the impression that you don't like him?'

'It's a long story,' Laura sighed.

'Well, there's plenty of time. You can tell me all about it while I drive you home.'

And Laura spent the next half hour telling him of her mother's whirlwind romance and the reservations she had about Stanley.

'I can see you have a problem with him but what is he really like?' Daniel said at last. 'When I knew your mum, she struck me as being pretty level-headed.'

'She used to be.' Laura sighed again. 'Perhaps it's her age — the change, you know. She keeps saying she wants some romance in her life before it's too late.' Laura wrinkled her nose. 'Not very nice to think about, is it? Old people like that . . . '

'Your mother isn't so old.'

'No, but Stanley is. He has skin like an old rhinoceros. He has to be sixty.'

'And is his great age the only thing you have against him?'

'Don't laugh at me, Daniel. I just feel he's not to be trusted. My mother takes everything he says at face value. He says he's in love with her and she believes it. I can't help feeling he has a hidden agenda, that's all.'

'Your mother's a big girl, Laura, and you can't live her life for her. If there's something not quite right with Stanley, she'll have to find it out for herself.'

'I know.' Laura looked out of the window, noticing the brown grass by the side of the road. 'What's happened here? Everything looks so dry.'

'The winter rains just didn't happen. Our

water levels have been dropping for over ten years. Yet more and more people want to settle in Melbourne and the sprawl of the suburbs goes on — '

Laura nodded, thinking of her own plans. Plans she had not yet confided to Daniel. Perhaps he already suspected that she was hoping to stay for good. That luggage must surely have given him a clue.

Recognizing the neighbourhood, she saw at last where he was taking her — to his town residence, his renovated mansion in Kew.

'I hope you won't mind me leaving you here for a bit,' he said. 'Mrs Wicks knows you're coming and will have made up the bed in the spare room.'

'We're not going down the peninsula, then?' she said, disappointed. She knew the Marlowe homestead was now the Morgans' primary home.

'Tomorrow maybe or the next day,' he said, as if reassuring her. 'Just not right now.'

'Everything is all right, Daniel? With you and Foxie?'

'Oh, it will be.' He frowned slightly, avoiding her gaze by keeping his eyes on the road. 'It's just that she's pregnant and — '

'Pregnant? Really? But that's wonderful news.'

'Yes, it is. Or it would be if she — '

'If nothing! I can be useful. I'll baby-sit for you. I'll knit baby clothes.'

'Laura, stop getting so excited and let me tell you. Foxie isn't best pleased.'

'She isn't? Why not?'

'She keeps saying it's happened too soon.'

'Well, I don't think so.' As usual, Laura said the first thing that came into her mind. 'She's pushing thirty, isn't she? So are you.'

'We're not quite in our dotage, thank you.' Daniel gave a wry smile. 'But she's sick most of the time and won't accept medication in case it's not good for the baby. It keeps her almost permanently in a rage.'

'And getting that excited can't be good for her blood pressure,' said Laura, who had had first-hand knowledge of the baby-hatching experiences of friends in Ireland.

'Exactly,' Daniel said. 'I'm so pleased you understand.'

By now, they had arrived at his house. Laura smiled up at the façade, familiar to her as she had stayed there before. 'The old place looks just the same.'

Mrs Wicks, Daniel's elderly housekeeper, heard their arrival and came to greet them, fussing over Laura and promising tea. Quickly, Daniel lifted the heavier of Laura's suitcases up to her room and then glanced at his watch.

44

'Sorry, Laura, I have to dash. Business calls. But you must be tired after your journey. Relax now and try to catch up on some sleep. I'll be back after six and we'll go out to dinner. Celebrate your arrival.'

'But what about Foxie? Won't she expect you home?'

He sighed. 'The best thing I can do for Foxie right now is stay out of her way. She blames me for her condition, you know.' He stopped Laura's next words with a finger against her lips. 'And don't buy into the argument. The doctor says she'll settle down when she gets used to it. And stops being sick, of course.'

'But — '

'Laura. Have Mrs Wicks's tea and then get some sleep. I'll be back for you some time after six.'

2

Flying the short distance from Sydney to Melbourne, Declan tried to erase all thought of Laura from his mind. Usually, he could trust his first impressions of people and found it hard to believe he had been so wrong about her. She had seemed so genuine, so sweet, and it had been a shock to find out she wasn't. She was nothing but an old-fashioned man-trap, a schemer like Lucy with nothing but marriage on her mind. A girl who would track down her unfortunate man and snare him with the precision of a fox stalking a rabbit. He gave a mild shudder, resolving to avoid the company of all women — at least for the duration of this trip with Lancelot's Pride. He would have enough to do making sure the gelding was fit and ready to be competitive enough to acquit himself well in this prestigious race. He didn't look forward to explaining the whys and wherefores to Tavis if not.

He didn't change his flight because he wished to avoid seeing Laura — that was an added bonus — but when he checked his messages, he found one from Jodie, informing him that the flight carrying Lance was due to arrive in Melbourne several hours before his own. Of course, transport to the quarantine stables had already been arranged and all she had to do was present the necessary paperwork to the authorities but she hated dealing with officials and would much prefer it if he could be there. Declan groaned. While Jodie was a good horsewoman and great with the animals, her people skills left much to be desired.

He passed through Customs easily, having little in the way of luggage, his passport and visa in order, and hurried to that part of the airport where Jodie and his horse were due to arrive. He could hear Jodie's voice raised in panic even before he caught sight of her.

'Can't we wait for Mr Martin? His flight should be in from Sydney any moment now. He did say he'd be here.'

'I am here, Jodie. What's the problem?'

'Oh, Declan, thank goodness,' she said, scarcely troubling to greet him. 'I've seen Lance and as far as I know, he seems to have travelled well — although we won't really know until he's weighed and — '

'Later, Jodie. Stop fussing and show the man the papers. Is that so hard? I want to get Lance settled in at Sandown soon as poss.'

'But there are several horse floats waiting

out there. I don't know which one is ours.'

'Then we'll ask.' Declan massaged an incipient headache, wishing he'd thought of his own comfort rather than that of Lancelot's Pride. Wes would have had the horse halfway to Sandown by now.

★　★　★

After a light lunch provided by Mrs Wicks before she left, Laura went to bed but although she rested, sleep evaded her. Her thoughts kept straying back to the time she had spent with Declan and her heart lurched again when she remembered his parting kiss.

Now you stop that, Laura Flanagan, she lectured herself. *It's not as if you've never been kissed before. Remember your purpose. A fellow Irishman is no good to you, even if he might be the love of your life!* Having been on the edge of a daydream, she was suddenly wide awake. What on earth had made her think that? Most likely she would never see Declan Martin again and that would be best for everyone. From now on, she would stay out of trouble and go about her purpose confiding in no one — except perhaps her friend Eileen at the Auld Irish Leprechaun pub.

Thinking of Eileen brought her to the

second part of her plan. Daniel and Foxie seemed to have problems enough, coming to terms with incipient parenthood. The last thing they needed was a visitor underfoot. Somehow she must find work and support herself while she searched for her Australian Mr Right. Twelve months might seem long enough now but in real terms, it wasn't. Tomorrow she must make a start on her new life. As these thoughts filtered through her mind, she drifted off to sleep.

'Laura! Wake up, sleepy head.' It seemed only five minutes since she dropped off but Daniel had returned and was shaking her out of a dream that she was still on the plane; she could even hear the drone of the engines. 'You can't sleep any longer now or you'll be awake in the early hours of the morning.'

'You're back already.' she mumbled, struggling to keep her eyes open.

'There's no 'already' about it. It's past seven o'clock. Hop in the shower now and find some clean clothes. I told you, we're going to a posh place to celebrate.'

'Daniel,' she said, swinging her legs out of bed and rubbing something that felt like grit from her eyes, 'Would you mind if we went to a café or something and saved the big celebration for the weekend? Then, if she feels up to it, maybe Foxie could join us and — '

'Sure.' He shrugged. 'There's a nice little Italian place round the corner. I often go there when I'm eating alone.'

'And does that happen often?' She gave him an anxious glance which he avoided.

'These days, more often than I'd like.'

'Oh, Daniel, I'm so sorry. You and Foxie seemed so perfect for each other, so — '

'Stop looking so tragic. We're not in the divorce courts just yet. And when she has two little red-headed horrors to run after, she won't have time to get mad at me.'

'Two?'

'Oh, didn't I tell you?' Daniel gave a lopsided grin. 'She was angry enough over getting pregnant with one child. She was fit to be tied when the doctor said it was twins.'

★　★　★

In spite of Jodie's unpromising start to their Australian visit, in the end Declan was pleased he had brought her. With his regular strapper to soothe and spoil him, Lancelot's Pride settled well in his new quarters, eating his regular feed — thoughtfully sent ahead by Tavis as there were regulations about that too. Apart from losing a kilo or so, he had suffered no ill effects from his journey. He viewed his new surroundings with curiosity, nostrils flaring as he sniffed the air, appearing to relish the unfamiliar scents of wattle and eucalypt as well as the luxury of his surroundings.

Declan was satisfied to see that both quarantine regulations and security were tight, realizing that for the first two weeks of their visit, he would be expected to keep away from the local horses and to wash and change his clothes after visiting his own horse in quarantine. Thankfully, Jodie seemed to be making new friends quickly among the other visiting stable hands and track riders and she wasn't relying on him for entertainment after hours.

Accommodation had been arranged for both of them at a motel not far from the course. Although he had a suite while Jodie had to make do with a single room, it was far from luxurious and the place didn't look as if it had been redecorated since the eighties. On the plus side, it smelled of nothing but fresh air and the linen was crisp and clean. Declan knew that while Tavis Martin had no choice but to pay for Lance's first-class stabling at Sandown, he would see no point in indulging his staff.

It didn't take him long to find out there was another visiting foreman, John Partridge, from a high-profile stables in England, staying at the same motel.

'The beds are comfortable enough.' His new friend grinned, wrinkling his nose. 'All we need is a place to crash — we don't have to hang around here to eat. You should sample the city's restaurants while you're in town — they're among the best in the world.'

'Are they?' Declan murmured. 'I'm new to this travellin' lark so I wouldn't know.'

'Stick with me then and I'll show you the sights. Look, don't be alone on Saturday night — me and some of the lads have a table booked at a Chinese restaurant — reputed to be the best. Why not join us? Get to meet everyone.'

'Oh, I don't know.' Declan hesitated; he wasn't a man for parties or crowds. 'Wouldn't like to intrude.'

'Don't be daft.' John wouldn't take no for an answer. 'We're all here for the same purpose — to pick off some of the prizes in the Spring Carnival. No reason we shouldn't enjoy ourselves at the same time.'

'OK, then. Why not?'

★　★　★

By the time Saturday evening came around, Laura was rested and ready for the celebration Daniel had originally planned for the first night of her arrival. She had got over her jet-lag and pushed her regrets about Declan to the back of her mind. Hoping to impress Daniel and Foxie with her new sophistication, she put on the new black and white dress her mother had bought for her before they parted in London.

'Can't go wrong with black and white.' Bridie had smiled, insisting that Laura should take it, in spite of the crippling price. 'Suitable for any occasion.' It was figure-hugging and had a neckline that plunged without being immodest and she wore it with a pair of high-heeled black patent sandals. She added more eye make-up than usual and brushed her dark hair into obedience, tucking it behind her ears. Looking at herself critically in the mirror, she hoped to do credit to her cousin and his wife.

She knew Daniel was spending most of Saturday morning in his office but she hoped he would have made time to drive down the coast and persuade Foxie to come back to town. She did her best to hide her disappointment when he turned up alone.

'No Foxie?' she said in a small voice. 'So when am I going to see her?'

Daniel shrugged, not quite meeting her gaze.

'She's not pleased that I'm back, is she?' Laura said intuitively, putting two and two together from Daniel's reaction. 'What is she thinking? That I'm going to get in the way and make extra work for her? Daniel, you know I'm not like that.'

'Yes, I do.' He sighed, looking awkward. 'Laura, I don't want you to take this personally. It's Foxie's problem, not yours. She isn't herself these days. It wouldn't matter if the Angel Gabriel himself descended from heaven with a flight of cleaning ladies — not even that would please her.'

'But — '

'Let it alone, Laura. It's best to let her get over this grouchy phase on her own.'

'Daniel, I don't think so. Alone, she'll just brood and get more miserable than ever.'

He ignored this remark and glanced at his watch. 'We should go. There's a lot of pressure for tables at this place. They won't hold the booking for more than five minutes if we're late.'

* * *

The restaurant was in Chinatown, one of Daniel's favourites, and Laura remembered visiting it before. On that occasion Foxie had been there, radiant with happiness and

54

glowing with health just after their honeymoon. But she didn't mention that now, not wanting to remind Daniel of happier times. She settled into her seat, smiling at the waiter who had escorted them to their table and presented them with enormous, comprehensive menus, bound with bright red cord and tassels. Laura glanced around the room, observing that most of the tables were already occupied.

'Busy,' she said.

'Always is. Every night,' he murmured, giving his attention to the menu. 'Now is there anything you fancy? What shall we have?'

'Oh, I'll leave it to you. I like everything, long as there's loads of fried rice.'

'Champagne then for starters.'

'Wouldn't it be more traditional to have green tea?'

'Yes but not as festive. This is a celebration, remember.'

The champagne was duly brought but instead of the cork popping discreetly from the bottle, as it did for most experienced wine waiters, it exploded with a loud bang, hitting one of the ceiling lights and making Laura shriek. For a few moments, their table was the centre of all attention until the waiter, full of apologies, offered to change their tablecloth and bring another bottle. When it arrived, Laura closed her eyes and winced, holding her breath in case the same thing should happen again. But this time the bottle was opened without mishap and they toasted each other before starting their meal.

In spite of doing justice to the delicious Chinese food, with liberal quantities of huge Australian prawns, Laura was tipsy and giggling after just one glass of the vintage champagne. In the midst of laughing wildly over something Daniel had said which was really not meant to be funny, she sensed that someone was watching her from across the room. She looked up, straight into Declan Martin's intense and critical gaze. She had never realized that those clear green eyes could look so wintry and cold, like tropical seas just before a storm. Her heart felt as if it had leaped in her chest and she felt herself blushing furiously. At last she forced herself to ignore him, looking away.

'What's the matter, Laura?' Daniel reached across the table to touch her hand. 'You've gone red as a turkey. Are you OK?'

'Sure'n I'm fine.' She gave a nervous laugh, pressing her hands to her burning face. 'It's a bit hot in here an' I'm not that used to drinkin' champagne. I'll be OK in a while.'

'Drink some water then; it'll dilute it and

make you feel better. I should've remembered that you're a one-pot screamer. D'you want me to ask for the bill, so we can leave?'

'No. You haven't had your pistachio ice cream and fritters.'

'Well, if you're sure.'

'I told you, I'm fine,' she said, smiling and moving her chair to avoid Declan's persistent stare. She changed the subject, turning Daniel's attention to something else.

'You're not goin' to be busy tomorrow now, are you, Daniel?'

'I don't know. I could spend an hour or so in the office — '

'But you don't have to?'

'No,' he said slowly, starting to get suspicious. 'Why? What did you have in mind?'

'I want you to take me down the coast to see what's going on with Foxie.'

He leaned back and sighed. 'I've already told you why that isn't a good idea.'

'I don't care if she bites my head off. I'd be happy for it if it makes her feel any better. She's having your babies, Daniel, and just because she's bad-tempered doesn't mean you should neglect her an' leave her down there in the country all on her own. No wonder she's getting depressed.'

'Now that's unfair — ' Daniel started to

say until he paused, as someone was looming over their table. Laura smiled, expecting it to be the waiter with their dessert. Instead, she looked up into Declan Martin's angry gaze. He was leaning in close enough to kiss but he didn't seem to have that in mind. She could feel her heart thumping so loudly, she thought he must hear it. How could she have forgotten how utterly gorgeous he was, especially wearing that dark green suede jacket which set off his coal-black hair and those green eyes, presently snapping with temper.

'You didn't let the grass grow under your feet, did you Laura?' he said in a low voice.

'Excuse me,' she whispered. He was so close, she could smell his after-shave; a corner of her mind noting it was delicious, making her want to close her eyes and breathe it in. 'I'm sure I don't know what you mean.'

'Oh, I think you do.' He glanced at Daniel and spoke in a stage whisper. 'Wealthy enough if a little bit old for you. How long d'you think it'll take you to get him to propose?'

'Now just a minute — ' Daniel's temper was also on the rise. 'I don't know who you think you are but you've no business coming here and upsetting my — '

'Oh, I know very well who I am, sir. An'

you don't have to get up, I'm leavin' now. All I'm sayin' is you should question this young lady's motives.' He saluted Daniel, blew Laura a mocking kiss and, satisfied he had put the cat among the pigeons, hurried to catch up with the rest of his party already leaving the room. Daniel frowned, watching him go.

'Who the hell is that?' he said when Declan was out of sight. 'And more Irish than Paddy McGinty's goat. An old boyfriend of yours?'

'No.' Laura looked down in her lap, miserable that Declan had gone off without giving her a chance to explain or to introduce Daniel as her cousin. Having jumped to the wrong conclusion, he must be thinking the worst of her. 'Just someone I met on the plane. He's bringing a horse to Melbourne to have a crack at the Melbourne Cup.'

'Well, I didn't like his style — not at all. You should be more careful who you talk to on these long journeys.'

'He was sitting right next to me, Daniel. What was I to do? Pretend to be a deaf mute?'

'Hmm.' Daniel considered it for a moment. 'He was behaving like someone who means a lot more to you than an acquaintance you met on a plane.'

'Well, he's not. And if you must know, I let my tongue run away with me. Told him too much about meself.'

'OK. What did you tell him?'

'Daniel, please. Don't give me the third degree. I'd rather not say.'

'Just tell me.' Daniel stood up, ready to give chase. 'Or I'll catch up with him outside and find out for myself.'

'Jus' sit down, please. It's nothin' really. Since we were both from Ireland, it was only natural that we should start talkin' an' he asked me what I was going to do with myself in Australia.'

'Right.' Daniel sat back and smiled at the waiter, more relaxed as the fritters and ice cream arrived. 'Well, I'd like to know that myself.'

'An' I told him I wanted to stay in Australia permanently — but in order to do that, I needed to marry an Aussie — '

Daniel spluttered, almost choking on a mouthful of ice cream. He managed to swallow it and laughed even more heartily, shaking his head. 'Laura, you're priceless,' he said when he sobered at last, wiping tears of mirth from his eyes.

'I'm glad you find it so amusing.' She bristled. 'Because I'm perfectly serious.'

Daniel rolled his eyes. 'Even so, how could the fellow get so offended by that?' He considered it for a moment. 'Unless of course . . . '

'Unless what?'

'Unless he was falling for you himself. That would explain it.'

'Oh, don't be ridiculous. You should have heard what he said — he was so rude. He supposed I'd be selling myself to the highest bidder, I was calculating and — what else was it? — oh yes, cheap. Does that sound to you like a man falling in love?'

'Yeah.' Daniel was still suppressing laughter. 'I'd say it was exactly that.'

'So what if he is? Declan's no use to me,' Laura wailed. 'I want to stay here in Australia and make a new life and he'll go back home to Ireland when the Carnival's over.'

'And I suppose you lost no time in pointing that out?'

'I don't think so. Not in so many words.'

'He got the picture, anyway. Never mind. We can do without a rabid Irish swain pursuing you all over the countryside.'

Laura giggled at the thought. 'Don't worry. I don't think there's very much chance of that.'

★ ★ ★

Outside, Declan caught up with John Partridge and his friends.

'The lads want to make a night of it — go

on to a club.' John grinned, jabbing him in the ribs. 'They've heard of some place where there's table-top dancers, all with Brazilians — '

'Thanks but no thanks, John. That's not really my scene.'

'Oh, go on, live dangerously for once. Who's to know? You're twelve thousand miles from home.'

'I'm tired, John. Thanks for asking me to join you tonight — the meal was jus' grand but right now I'd rather go back to the motel and crash.'

'We could drop you off before we go on to the club.'

'No need to wreck your evening. I'll get a cab.'

'I know what's the matter with you, sonny.' John gave him a friendly punch on the shoulder. 'You want to lie in bed and pine for your pretty little brunette.'

John was joking but he didn't know how close to the truth he was. Declan did indeed want to spend some time analyzing his feelings for Laura. He had been surprised by the rage he'd felt to see her drinking champagne and laughing, having a whale of a time with that suave red-haired man; a typical suit. But what had possessed him to go up to their table and make such a scene? That wasn't like him at all. He had to remind himself and not for the first time that Laura was her own woman and whatever she chose to do with her life, it was no business of his. The thought didn't cheer him.

★ ★ ★

The following morning, in spite of Daniel's half-hearted objections, Laura insisted that he should drive her to Mornington to see Foxie. *En route*, she made him stop at a week-end florist to buy expensive, out-of-season flowers, piling bunches of exotic pink liliums, hothouse roses and multi-coloured freesias into his arms.

'Laura, this is far too much,' he protested. 'She'll think I've been having an affair.'

'Good,' she said. 'Let her worry a little. Maybe she'll start appreciating what she has.'

They piled the flowers into the back seat of his Mercedes and set off for the coast. Even at this early hour the roads were quite busy.

'Now,' Daniel said as they drove through the suburbs, leaving the city behind, 'I want to know exactly what has been going on inside that curly, dark head of yours. Tell me your plans.'

'I already did.' She shot him an anxious glance. 'To stay in Australia permanently, I need to fall in love and get married — '

'No, actually. You don't. You can apply for citizenship and I'll sponsor you.'

'I know. But that's the long way round it. I might even have to leave and come back later and I'm sure my new step-daddy's not up for that. No. My way will be quicker. I've already talked to a friend who can get me work at an Irish pub — '

'Laura, hold it right there. Your idea of marriage is crazy enough but you're not yet a resident. If you try to work, they'll deport you.'

'Who will?'

'Immigration, of course.' Daniel rolled his eyes, exasperated. 'They're hot on such things these days.'

'And how are they going to find out? I worked when I was here before — nothing happened then.'

'I never knew that. Doing what?'

'Aha, you see? You don't know everything. I worked in a vintage clothing store for a month or so, covering for a friend.'

'Well, you were lucky to get away with it.'

She pulled a face at him. 'Don't be such a grump. And don't worry, I've no intention of being a burden to you or to Foxie. I can share a flat near the pub with some other girls.'

Daniel fell silent, not knowing what else to say. His young cousin appeared so confident, so sure that her plans would work out, that he didn't want to wade in with the big boots of reality and trample her dreams.

3

Because of what Daniel had told her, Laura had been expecting Foxie to look different; less glamorous maybe, less assured and maybe even a little bloated in pregnancy. It was a surprise, therefore, to walk into the homestead and find Foxie very much as she'd last seen her, having tea and toast in the kitchen. She laughed, seeing Daniel standing in the doorway, half hidden by Laura's mountain of flowers.

'Daniel, what on earth did you do?' Her voice was deep and humorous, reminding Laura how much sexier a woman's voice sounded in the lower register. 'It must have been something awful to merit so many flowers.'

'There you are,' he said to Laura as he handed them to his wife with a peck on her cheek. 'I told you she'd think the worst.'

Foxie put them all in the sink and turned on water to give them a drink before greeting Laura.

'Laura, how lovely to see you.' She pulled the younger woman into her arms to give her a quick embrace. 'I'm afraid I owe you an apology.'

'Whatever for?'

'I must have sounded less than welcoming when we talked. I'm sorry but I'd just had rather a shock, being told I was pregnant and with twins.'

'You're not pleased?'

'I wasn't at first. But the idea is starting to grow on me.' She sighed. 'And the babies are going to grow in me whether I like it or not.'

'But that's good news, isn't it? Getting half your family all in one go?'

'Half of it?' Foxie looked appalled. 'Laura, believe me. This is all the family I'm ever going to have.'

'Come on, love, don't get excited,' Daniel warned. 'Remember what the doctor said about blood pressure.'

'And don't you patronize me,' she fired back, fixing him with an eagle's glare. 'I'm not one of your brood mares.'

'OK. OK.' He held up his hands in surrender. 'Everything I say seems to annoy you these days. I'll go and check out Jim at the stables.' And, whistling to cover his discomfiture, he thrust his hands in his pockets and left.

Laura had watched the exchange and was now biting her lip, unsure what to say. Daniel and Foxie had been so in love but now, it seemed, they were losing their way.

'Sorry again, Laura.' Foxie seemed close to tears. 'You didn't come all this way to see that and I haven't even offered you a cup of tea.'

'I'll get it.' She got up at once, relieved to have something to do.

Fortunately, lunch was much better. Laura helped Foxie to make soup and sandwiches and Daniel returned from the stables in a good mood, pleased with what he had seen there. Foxie herself made an effort to be more cheerful and was able to eat some lunch, not feeling so sick today. Afterwards, when she excused herself, saying she needed a rest, Daniel once more raised the subject of Laura's plans.

'I wish you'd just take some time to relax and enjoy yourself,' he said. 'You really don't need to work. Why not look on it as a gap year?'

'But Daniel, I want to work and I promise it'll be all right. I can share rooms with some other girls, almost next door to the pub, so I won't have to travel about late at night. And they're short-handed so they want me to start tomorrow.'

He sighed and she knew he was searching for some reasonable way to put her off such a course.

'Laura,' he said at last, 'get real. If you're caught working on a visitor's visa, you'll be deported at once — you do realize that? And if that happens, the authorities will make it twice as difficult for you to return.'

'I won't get caught. There's loads of Irish girls working there and they don't have any trouble with the law — '

'No. Because they have proper permission to live and work here. You don't. Didn't the publican ask to examine your work permit?'

'No.' Laura ran her hands down her jeans, refusing to meet his gaze. She didn't want to confess that Eileen had given her somebody else's, a girl by the name of Emerald Green; a name so unusual, it couldn't possibly be real. And Patrick had scarcely glanced at it although he did call her Em. She'd have to remember, when she was working, that that was her name. 'And anyway I'll soon have a real one of my own. If I can marry an Australian, I'll be able to stay.'

'Laura! Don't you realize how hopelessly naïve that sounds? Why not go through the proper channels and let us sponsor you?'

'Daniel, I appreciate the thought but that takes forever. I'd have to go back to Ireland to wait for all the paperwork to come through and I can't afford to. And, if I did, I'd have to live with old Auntie Kit whose house always smells of boiled cabbage.' Laura shuddered. 'No. I'd rather marry an Aussie and then I won't have to leave here at all.'

'Just a minute. Let me get something straight. Are you saying you're going to throw yourself at the head of the first man who'll have you?'

'Oh no. Or I'd have taken up with Barry Glenn.'

'Over my dead body,' Daniel snapped. Although Barry Glenn was a friend and a business associate, he was a much married television presenter and at least twice Laura's age.

All the same, having done his best to dissuade her, Daniel had respected her wishes and done nothing further to prevent her from joining her new friends and going to work at the pub.

★ ★ ★

It was late afternoon and getting busy at the Auld Irish Leprechaun. As one of the most popular Irish public houses in Melbourne, it had the added benefit of being close to the newly renovated Flemington Racecourse and was the favoured haunt of Irish immigrants as well as many of the well-known faces in the local horse-racing industry. Patrick James, who owned and managed it, knew his clientele. He kept the place friendly and just a little scruffy so that the horsemen would feel comfortable enough to come in straight from the stables. The only glamour it had was behind the bar.

The Leprechaun, with its cheerful, slightly old-fashioned sign depicting a mischievous imp with his arms round a pot of gold, had a genuine feel to it: It wasn't like one of those Americanized Irish pubs where the brass had been polished until it shone like glass, the ceilings were painted brown to represent old smoke, the seats were uncomfortable benches and there were whimsical sayings on wooden plaques, hanging at odd angles on all the walls. No. The Leprechaun was a straightforward, old-fashioned Irish pub with seats at the bar and alcoves with comfortable armchairs where groups of friends could congregate almost in private. A place unafraid to be caught smelling of Guinness and beer.

And, with the Spring Carnival just a matter of weeks away, the balloons and decorations were already up and excitement building, along with speculation about the final line-up for the Melbourne Cup.

Laura Flanagan had been working there for just over a month now. As well as enjoying the work, she found it perfect for meeting people and had already gone out on several first dates. Unfortunately, they hadn't led any-where and she was still far away from finding her Mr Right. She reminded herself she had much less than a year left to meet and marry him. *I mustn't think about it so much,* she thought. *Men have a sixth sense about such things — they can smell desperation. It'd be like going around with a neon sign over my head saying 'Bridegroom wanted'.*

'Come on, Dolly Daydream!' Her friend Eileen gave her quite a painful jab in the ribs as she stood behind the bar. 'Let's be havin' you. There's a guy over there with an empty pot and his tongue hanging out. Are you going to serve him or not?'

'Sorry.' Laura murmured, giving the customer her most dazzling smile as she went to refill his glass. She was wearing a new cherry-red dress that made her skin glow and flattered her abundant dark hair. She was very conscious of his admiring glance.

As she was filling several more glasses with Guinness, there was laughter and a commo-tion at the door as a party of Irish horsemen came in, bringing with them strong smells of hay and the stables.

'They might at least have a shower before they come in here,' Eileen grumbled, wrinkling her nose. But Laura liked horses and horsemen; such smells reminded her of

Daniel and Foxie's place on the coast.

'What shall it be, lads?' She smiled at them. 'Guinness all round?'

Some nodded while others expressed interest in trying the local brew.

Turning away from them, Laura began the slow process of pouring Guinness, waiting for the foam to settle as the glasses filled. She sensed the door opening behind her as two more people came in.

'Oh my God,' Eileen whispered beside her, tossing her mop of red curls. 'I think I've died and gone to heaven. Don't look now but he's just walked in. The most beautiful man in the world.'

'Eileen!' Laura giggled. 'With you this happens at least twice a day.' All the same, she turned to glance at the supposed paragon, surprised to find herself looking into Declan Martin's equally startled gaze.

'Laura?' he said uncertainly, unsure how she would treat him after their last encounter at the restaurant. 'What on earth are you doing here?'

'Working.' She smiled, wishing she didn't feel so ridiculously pleased to see him.

'On a visitor's visa?' He murmured, making her glance around to see if Patrick were listening. During that moment of inattention, he captured her left hand and saw it was still empty of rings. 'And still not engaged?' he said almost gleefully.

She snatched her hand away. 'Stop it, Declan. Do you have to keep goin' on about that? It was only a joke, that's all. A stupid joke.'

'Really?' he said. 'I'm sure you meant it at the time.'

Out of the corner of her eye, Laura could see Patrick sizing up the situation through narrowed eyes. Suddenly, she was all business. 'So what'll it be, lads?'

'Two pints of Guinness please, miss.' Declan picked up his cue at once. 'And make it snappy, would you? We've a thirst above rubies here.' And immediately, he turned his back on her to talk to his friend.

'Let me do it,' Eileen insisted eagerly. 'You're still busy with those other guys.'

Laura nodded, topped up the four other Guinnesses and presented them to the men waiting for them at the other end of the bar.

Declan took his revenge by flirting with Eileen. 'And what's a lovely colleen like you doin' here such a long way from home?' he teased.

'I'm not a long way from home at all,' she said, still with a lilting Southern Irish accent. 'My parents are Irish but I was born here. It's just that Patrick likes us to sound authentic.

Says it adds to the atmosphere.'

Listening with scant attention, he glanced past her looking for Laura, who was serving another customer, studiously avoiding his gaze. 'But that other girl — Laura — she's the real thing, isn't she? How long has she been working here?'

'Ssh!' Eileen gave a quick glance around to see if anyone overheard. 'Here she doesn't go by that name. Far as Patrick's concerned, she's called Em. Emerald Green.'

Declan gave a bark of laughter. 'How very apt. It suits her.'

Eileen pursed her lips, searching for something that would draw his attention back to herself. 'Never mind her. I'd rather talk about you. Here for the Carnival, are you? Got a hot tip for the Melbourne Cup?'

'No, I haven't.' Declan grinned. 'People keep asking that but I don't know anythin' about the other runners at all. Just Lancelot's Pride — my uncle's horse.'

'Lancelot's Pride. That's a fancy name,' Eileen teased. 'I'll have to see if there's a runner called Guinevere. She'll bring him down.'

Declan smiled but Eileen could see she had only half his attention. And, after that, although he was a frequent visitor to the Auld Irish Leprechaun, he kept his distance from

Laura and, in spite of Eileen's broad hints, never asked her to go out. He seemed happy to spend half an hour or so just watching the pair of them and, after his pint of Guinness, which he nursed for the full half hour, he never ordered anything else.

'What is it with you and Declan?' Eileen asked Laura one night as they were clearing the bar before going home. 'Although he avoids you, it's you he's interested in — not me. I've been watching him when he thinks no one's looking and his eyes follow you all round the room. It's like there's some undercurrent, an attraction flowing between you but neither one of you will make the first move.'

'Declan's no use to me, Eileen, an' he knows it. If I want to stay in Australia permanently, I'll have to marry someone who lives here.'

'So, is staying here more important than meeting the love of your life?'

'The love of my life, indeed.' Laura sneered. 'I'm not sure there's any such thing. You've been reading too many cheap novels.'

'I'm too busy to read. I haven't the time.'

'Seeing stupid, happy-ever-after movies then. If Declan thinks he wants me, it's only because he knows he can't have me. Now then, I want to know all about this barbecue at your cousin's place in the hills. I hope she has lots of single, male Australian friends.'

'Yeah,' Eileen said, slowly shaking her head. 'But no one in the same class as your Declan.'

'Oh, stop it, Eileen. For the last time, he isn't my Declan and never will be.'

★ ★ ★

The barbecue was to be held at a small but picturesque house, high up in the Dandenongs and surrounded by gum trees. Driven by Eileen, who owned a nippy Toyota, Laura hadn't been to the hills before. Surprised by how quickly the suburban sprawl gave way to the forest, she was amazed at how green it was; the fern trees by the roadside, spreading like huge umbrellas and the tall mountain ash, some hundreds of years old, stretching towards the sky. Invisible birds sang their exotic songs and occasionally crimson rosellas, in a flash of bright red and blue plumage, would pass overhead, screaming raucously as they flew.

After a few more miles, Eileen turned off the road into a steep, unmade driveway. Laura bit her lips, trying not to show her anxiety as the little vehicle struggled to cover the uneven ground to reach the plateau above. She was relieved when the car stopped outside a sprawling, ranch-style log cabin with a large, covered veranda outside.

Well past midday, the party was in full swing. Music and outdoor cooking smells reached them as soon as they left the car and Laura's stomach rumbled. Eileen's cousin, Irene, descended on them with a shriek of welcome and a hug.

'Eileen! You made it. And this must be Laura. Very glam,' she said, taking in Laura's red dress. Laura smiled but she wished Eileen had told her it would be casual dress. Everyone else was in jeans, sweaters or shirts and she felt conspicuous and overdressed in her figure-revealing red jersey.

Someone thrust a glass of white wine into her hand and she sipped it cautiously, taking stock of the other guests, about twenty people in all. Many of them were obviously couples, some with small babies strapped in harnesses to their chests. There were several grand-mothers balanced precariously on plastic chairs in the shade of a large gum tree, doing their best to deal with what looked like burned chops and chunks of bread, dripping with grease, making Laura think perhaps she wasn't so hungry, after all. Sighing, she turned away, looked at the other end of the veranda and saw him. He was so perfect, for a moment she couldn't breathe. Tall but not too tall, he was slender and wearing what could only be expensive designer jeans, his belt buckle glinting silver as it caught the sun. The sleeves of his shirt were rolled back to reveal light brown hands and arms covered in fine, golden hairs. He was tanned but in a way that looked expensive; a beach tan rather than that of someone who worked out of doors. His fair hair was golden tipped and so carelessly barbered it must have cost a fortune. Cowboy boots completed the picture. She wanted to ask Eileen who he was but Eileen had already moved on, talking and laughing with people who were obviously old friends.

Colin saw her staring at him from across the room, her beautiful dark blue eyes taking in every inch of him. She was new and that interested him. This party might turn out not to be so boring after all. He raised an eyebrow and gave her a quirky smile to show her that he was aware of her interest. She blushed to a tone almost matching her sexy red dress and immediately avoided his gaze. He laughed inwardly. Not so hard-boiled then. Good. And she was definitely his type; well rounded without being too plump and with that gorgeous mass of dark hair. He felt himself harden, imagining it spilling across his arms as she lay naked in his bed, surrendering to his embrace.

'Eileen, me love.' He crooked a finger, beckoning her. 'Aren't you going to introduce me to your friend?'

Laura couldn't believe her good fortune. Once introduced, he had stayed by her side the whole afternoon, appearing to hang on her every word. After that first glass of wine, she had stuck to mineral water, anxious to create a good impression. He asked her how long she had been in Australia and if she had family here. She told him all about her mother and Stanley Winton but not about Daniel and Foxie. Somehow she sensed he preferred to think she didn't have relatives in Australia.

Apart from his name, Colin Newbold, she learned little about him or his background. His father was in transport, he said, and he himself liked computers. As the afternoon wore on, she was almost holding her breath, waiting for him to ask to see her again.

Well aware of this, Colin decided to let her stew. He would play his fish a little longer before reeling her in. By the time they did get together, she would be panting for his kisses, like a plum, ripe and ready to fall into his hands. He had told her as little about himself as he could and certainly not about his projected engagement to Jill.

Of course Jill wasn't in love with him any more than he was with her. But it was what both sets of parents wanted and he knew that if they got married, the rewards would be great; the son of the transport magnate and the daughter of the man famous for his chain of electronic appliance stores. Jill's father was willing to buy them any house that she wanted and his own father had promised him that silver sports coupé as a special wedding gift.

But he wasn't going to let these commitments cramp his style — he wasn't ready to tie the knot just yet. And, as luck would have it, he had something on Jill. He had caught her at home in the shower stall attached to the swimming pool — with the pool boy of all people. What a cliché. They were almost done when Jill had seen him standing there watching them. She had run after him with a towel wrapped around her dripping body, begging him not to tell. He wouldn't, of course, not unless it suited him. But it was amazing what she let him get away with after that.

As the afternoon gave way to evening, the party guests started to leave, driving carefully down the precarious drive and sounding car horns as they reached the road. Laura willed Colin to talk about meeting again but he didn't. Then Eileen was touching her shoulder, saying she was ready to leave. Laura murmured her thanks to the cousin who was tired now and suppressing yawns, wanting everyone to be gone. Colin strolled with the two girls towards Eileen's car.

'Bye, then.' He smiled into Laura's eyes as she leaned back against the car door. She tried to smile back, hoping he couldn't see her disappointment. At the last minute as Eileen, already revving the engine, was waiting for Laura to get in, he whipped a card out of his pocket and gave it to her. 'My mobile,' he whispered, almost kissing her ear. 'Call me soon.'

Clutching his card to her bosom as if he had given her a precious jewel, Laura was too overcome to be scared by the steep, uneven journey to the main road.

'Did you see that?' she whispered. 'He gave me his card. He wants me to call him.'

'Col Newbold?' Eileen gave her a sideways glance and then grunted, shaking her head. 'You'll be crazy if you do.'

4

Had Laura been allowed to do as she pleased, she would have called Colin's mobile the very next day but Eileen strongly advised against it. They were doing the morning shift at the Leprechaun and it was unusually quiet before the lunch-hour rush. Finding the precious card to make sure she hadn't lost it, Laura raised the subject yet again.

'Good Lord.' Eileen rolled her eyes and sighed. 'Let the man take a breath. If I were you, I'd throw his card away and forget him. But if you must go chasing after Mr 'Tickets-on-Himself' Col Newbold, you don't want to look too eager.'

Laura frowned. 'And I don't want him to think I'm not interested either.'

'Oh, I don't think there's much chance of that — you ogling him all afternoon with those big, blue, baby-doll eyes.'

'I wasn't. Ogling him, I mean.'

'You practically had your tongue hanging out.'

'I didn't. And you saw him. He followed me around all afternoon.' She considered her friend for a moment, head on one side.

'Eileen, are you sure you don't fancy him, just a little bit, for yourself?'

'Me? No thanks. I learned my lesson with Col Newbold when my cousin first brought him home about ten years ago.'

'Your cousin went out with him? You never said.'

'No. They were just part of the same gang at school. Old man Newbold didn't believe in private education. He needed Col in the transport business — didn't want him to get any fancy ideas about going to uni or something. So he sent him along to the local state school with us.'

'And you didn't like him?'

'No. He teased us mercilessly and never had a kind word for anyone. Only my cousin seemed to find it amusing. I promise you, Laura, he's selfish to the core. Doesn't care about anyone but himself.'

'That's not the impression he gave me.'

'Fine. If you're such a great judge of character, go right ahead. But don't say I didn't warn you.' And Eileen stomped off to the other end of the bar, ready to serve the first lunch-hour customers coming in.

All the same, Laura took her friend's advice, containing her patience until almost the end of the week. Daniel had given her two good tickets to get into Caulfield Racecourse on Saturday for the Caulfield Cup. She planned to invite Colin to go with her and practised what she would say in front of the bathroom mirror.

Hi Colin, it's Laura from Sunday, remember? No. That was implying he might have forgotten her.

Hi Colin, it's Laura. How's tricks? How's tricks? Where on earth did that come from? It made her sound older than her mother.

In the end, she said, 'Hi, it's Laura,' deciding to let him take it from there. All the same, he acted mystified for a moment, making her think he had indeed forgotten her.

'Oh, oh *that* Laura. Yes, darling, how are you? Recovered from that woeful barbecue yet?'

'I didn't think it was woeful at all. Nor did you at the time.'

'Ah, well. Sometimes you see things differently after the dust settles.'

He didn't want to see her again. He was regretting giving her his card.

Nevertheless, she plunged on. How many girls could offer a man good seats in the grandstand on a major race day? Stumbling over her words, she managed to tell him what she had in mind.

'A day at the races?' He seemed to consider

it for a moment. 'Sorry, darling, I'm not much of a punter. 'Tisn't really my scene.'

'Oh,' she said, trying not to let him hear her disappointment as he kept her hanging on in silence for several seconds.

'But tell you what,' he said at last. 'I could do Friday night.'

'I can't. My shift doesn't finish till ten o'clock.'

'That's OK. I'll come round the pub. Pick you up. Leprechaun, isn't it? Same as Eileen?'

'Yes, oh yes. See you then.' And Laura hung up quickly, half afraid he would change his mind. She would be tired but that didn't matter. There were still lots of things you could do late on a Friday night. Go clubbing, maybe. Take in a midnight movie. She should have asked him what they were doing and whether to dress casually or not. She thought of ringing him back and decided against it.

Almost counting the hours until Friday night, she spent ages deciding what to wear. She looked out the black and white dress she had chosen with her mother in London, deciding it looked too formal for the cinema, even for clubbing. Seeing it again made her think of that last carefree afternoon and remembered with a jolt that it was months now since she had heard from Bridie — not even that she had arrived safely in New York.

She knew they were visiting Stan's relatives before flying south but they must have arrived at his home in Florida now? Surely Bridie could have dropped her a postcard? She herself had sent dozens of e-mails, some of them lengthy, telling Bridie all about her life in Australia and about Daniel and Foxie with their expectation of twins, of her friendship with Eileen and how she was enjoying her job at the Irish pub. But so far there had been no reply. Not one. And it wasn't like her — as a rule, Bridie was a prolific letter writer. Surely that man had to have an office or at least a connection to the internet in that mansion of his? Worry nagged her. What did they really know about Stanley? Only what he had told them. He might not be a wealthy landowner at all but a serial wife-killer who buried his victims in the swamp. Now she was letting her imagination run away with her. The next time she saw Daniel, she would confide her worries and ask him what to do.

Returning to the issue of her date with Colin, she thought it likely that he would be wearing jeans. As her own were beginning to look rather well worn, she splashed out on a pair of figure-hugging black trousers and an equally expensive short-sleeved cashmere sweater with a modest round neckline. Nothing like cashmere to add a bit of class, her mother always said. Then, considering all that black might look a bit funereal, she added a black leather belt, the buckle twinkling with rhinestones, highlighting her small waist. And from the admiring glances she drew from the customers during the early part of the evening at the pub, she knew she had chosen well and was looking good.

But half past nine came and went with no sign of Colin. Her mobile remained stubbornly silent and there was no text message explaining his absence. Even at ten o'clock when she and Eileen finished their shift, he still hadn't arrived. She made herself busy, wiping the bar, refusing to meet Eileen's gaze. A lump of misery settled in her chest as they said goodnight to Patrick and one or two regulars and she headed for the door. This was really too hard to bear. She had been living the last two days in anticipation of this evening and now it was all for nothing. Colin had found something better to do.

'Just don't say anything — don't!' she muttered to Eileen, almost unable to see where she was going, through eyes suddenly blinded by tears.

'I wasn't going to,' Eileen said. 'Except that Col Newbold is over there waving at us from one of his father's Mercedes. Posh.'

'Oh!' Laura breathed, quickly blinking

away her tears as she hurried towards him, scarcely remembering to wish Eileen good-night.

'You take care now,' Eileen called after her. 'Don't let him — '

But her warning fell on deaf ears. Laura's heart was singing again. He had remembered and all was right with the world. 'Why are you waiting out here in the cold?' she said. 'You should've come inside.'

He shrugged. 'Nah. Pubs aren't really my scene.' He looked her up and down, taking in the new clothes as he opened the door of his car for her and handed her in. 'Very tasty,' he murmured, close to her ear and making her smile.

Laura's pleasure in the luxury surrounding her lasted only a few minutes. It was a powerful car and she clung to her seat, trying not succumb to panic as Colin took to the motorway, weaving in and out of the traffic, flashing his lights at anyone in his path, driving recklessly and too fast.

'Where — where are we going?' she tried to ask.

'Nowhere special. Just a little place I know.'

'Is it a club — or — '

'Good God, no.' He gave her a pained glance. 'That's not my scene at all. Wouldn't have thought it was yours.'

Laura was surprised to feel a tickle of irritation as she looked at his profile, seeing for the first time that he had an unattractive, petulant twist to his lips. Not so good-looking after all then. He didn't like horse racing, didn't like dancing, didn't like pubs — how many more of the things she enjoyed were *not his scene*?

He turned from the motorway and pulled up outside a rather ordinary-looking motel. It didn't seem to promote any entertainment and was mostly in darkness, except for the booking office, which was still open with a clerk at the desk. Saying nothing to Laura, Colin sprang out of the car, leaving the door wide open and the motor running as he went to talk to the man inside. She saw him grin and give Colin a playful punch on the shoulder. They seemed to be old friends.

'Usual room, Col,' she thought she heard him say as he tossed him the key.

Laura's heart lurched but with dismay rather than pleasure. Naïve and unsophisticated she might be, but she wasn't entirely stupid. She knew exactly what Colin was doing. They scarcely knew one another — hadn't even kissed — yet he had driven her to this motel for the sole purpose of having sex.

Colin got back into the car grinning, gave a broad wink confirming her worst fears and drove to a unit at the far end of the block. There he switched off the engine and looked at her properly, registering her less-than-happy expression. He took hold of a strand of her hair and tugged it, none too gently.

'Come on, sweetie.' His whisper was almost a hiss in the gloom of the car. 'What's up? This is what you wanted, isn't it? A place where we can be alone?'

'I thought we were going somewhere we could get to know one another — have coffee maybe.'

He jerked his head towards the unit. 'Where better to get to know one another than in a motel room, away from prying eyes? And I'm sure there'll be coffee if you want it.'

Laura took a deep breath, trying not to show him how upset and scared she was.

'Colin, I'm sorry if I gave you the wrong impression. But this is not what I want. If you're not going to take me out to a public place then I'd rather go home.'

'Oh, OK. I get it.' He put his left arm round her shoulder and pulled her quite roughly towards him. 'You girls are all the same. Can't do anything without all the kisses and cuddles first. Here goes, then.' And suddenly, she was trapped in his arms, his mouth grinding against hers, his right hand kneading her left breast before finding the nipple and pinching it hard. It was painful, even through several layers of clothes.

This wasn't going as she had imagined it and she could sense his impatience and anger simmering just below the surface. His breath wasn't exactly bad but not entirely without odour and there was far too much tongue and saliva involved for a satisfactory first kiss. It made her feel more than a little sick. She pushed him away and broke free with a cry of disgust, turning her back on him to open her purse, searching for a tissue to wipe her face.

'Now,' she said, unable to keep the tremor from her voice, 'Are you taking me home or not?'

Acting as if he hadn't heard her, he sat back, watching her through narrowed eyes. 'Laura, tell me. Just how sexually experienced are you? I hope at least you've had a Brazilian before we get down to brass tacks?'

'A — a what?'

'A wax treatment.' He pronounced the words as if talking to an imbecile. 'So you can wear a very small bikini without showing hairs. If there's anything I can't stand, it's a woman with hair on her body.'

'No, I haven't,' she said, shocked by his candour. 'I don't wear a bikini. And I have no intention of letting you see me naked. Not tonight or any other.'

He started to laugh weakly. 'Oh, what a fool I am,' he said, shaking his head. 'I should've known. It's nothing but a little Irish virgin fresh from the convent — she's been told to jam her legs together and hold out for the wedding night. Oh no, sweetie, I'm afraid you don't catch me like that.'

'I don't want to catch you at all,' Laura shouted back at him. Now he had shown his true colours, she didn't even like him. Eileen had been right about everything. Luckily, fear was now giving way to outrage. Although she despised him, she was no longer scared. 'I just need you to drive me home.'

'Oh no, darl, I don't think so,' he drawled. 'I've wasted quite enough time on you already.' He leaned across her to fling open the door. 'Out you go.'

'But I can't.' She felt angry and at the same time close to tears. 'It's late and I've no idea where I am. How am I to get home?'

'Your problem, not mine. Get a cab.' He started the engine and made it roar, not caring who was disturbed by it. Lights went on in several units, and some people peered through the curtains, wondering what the noise was about. 'Get out! Now!' Colin snarled, pushing her none too gently towards the open door.

Glaring at him and trying to muster what remained of her dignity, Laura got out and slammed the door hard enough to rattle the glass. Colin gunned the Mercedes back to the motel office where he stopped with a squeal of brakes. Leaving the engine running yet again, he ran inside, flung the key at the man behind the counter and then, with screaming tyres and a bow-wave of gravel, took off towards the main road.

Laura's tears of relief didn't come until she was sure he had gone, although at first they didn't seem like tears of relief as she was shaken by great hiccupping sobs. She was feeling a mass of conflicting emotions. Disappointment in Colin — that he wasn't the white knight she had hoped for — but at the same time there was relief that she hadn't let him usher her into that bedroom; goodness knows what might have happened then. Having gone with him willingly, she could hardly turn round and protest she was raped.

She was shivering and crying, thoroughly chilled, having come out without a jacket. She leaned against the building, shock settling in. She knew she would have to wait until she could stop crying and was sufficiently composed to call a cab. Vaguely, she was aware of people coming towards her.

'Hey, there.' It was a gente female voice as

94

a girl put a hand on her arm., 'Did ye have a row with the boyfriend, then? He seemed a bit mad. Are ye all right?'

'Yes. Yes, I'm fine.' She was trying to smile through her tears but the effort was too great. 'No. Actually, I'm not.' Her mouth turned down and she cried like a child, nose streaming and tears rolling down her cheeks.

'Ah, dear now,' the girl said. 'Sure an' it can't be that bad.' Her sympathy only made Laura cry harder.

'Laura? Laura, is that you?' Suddenly, there was a voice she recognized. Declan. In her misery, she had scarcely noticed the Irish accent of his companion, it had seemed so normal to her. He put an arm around her and it felt so safe, so good. 'What's happened to you and who was that bastard? If he's hurt you, I swear I'll find him and I'll — '

'No. No, I'm fine. He was a bit put out because I — er — didn't want to — ' And she nodded towards the still vacant unit at the end of the row, brushing away her tears on the back of her hand.

'Well, thank God we found you. You're in safe hands now. And you look as if you could do with a strong cup of tea.' He guided her towards his suite, motioning the other girl to come with them. Inside he introduced them. 'Laura, this is Jodie, Lancelot's strapper.

She's staying here too.'

'With you?' Laura asked, wondering why that should make her feel miserable. After the encounter with Colin, nothing would have surprised her.

'Certainly not.' Jodie blushed to the roots of her carroty hair. 'Declan's just the boss. I have me own room. Me own life.'

'Sorry.' Laura murmured, feeling wretched again.

Fifteen minutes later, having drunk the scalding sweet tea provided by Jodie and wearing one of her jackets which smelled comfortingly of horse and hay, Declan suggested driving her home.

'I could get a cab,' she said half-heartedly. 'You have to be up early, don't you? With the horse.'

'Not that early. Jodie can start without me.' He raised his eyebrows at the girl, who nodded. 'Come on. You look all in.'

Laura found Declan's hired car comfortingly plain and middle class. She'd had quite enough of fast men in powerful cars. His driving was a comfort to her as well. He drove within the speed limits, and stayed in the middle lane, changing only as they left the motorway to avoid the tolls.

At first he didn't question her further about Colin or issue any warning that she had

96

been foolhardy to get into his car without knowing exactly where they would be going. Instead, he chatted easily about the differences he found between Irish and Australian flat racing and how pleased he was with the progress of Lancelot's Pride. In no time at all, they were parking outside the rambling apartment block where Laura shared a flat with her friends. She looked up at their windows, already in darkness.

'I'd ask you to come in for coffee,' she said hesitantly, 'but — '

'That's OK.' he said. 'I think you've had quite enough excitement for one night. But Laura — '

She took a deep breath and braced herself. Here it was. Here came the lecture — the *I told you so.*

'What were you doing with that hellion? The guy at the Chinese restaurant might've been a bit old for you but you seemed to be getting on so well together?'

'We do,' Laura laughed. 'But you didn't stay long enough to let me explain. I told you I had a cousin in Melbourne — that's him! And you should see his wife — she's just gorgeous. She used to star in an American soap.'

'Really? And gave it all up for love?'

'Sort of. It was a bit more complicated than that.' She could see that Declan wasn't really paying attention — he had something else on his mind.

'Laura, I think you need to slow down a bit. Give it a chance to happen naturally, this falling in love thing. It's not something you can force or even choose.'

'I do know, Declan. I realize that now. Thank you so much for bringing me home.'

'Take care, then.' He brushed a strand of hair away from her face and gave her a quick kiss on the cheek. 'I'll pop into the Leprechaun. See you soon.'

All of a sudden, she didn't want him to be gone. 'You could see me tomorrow, if you like,' she said impulsively. 'I know it's short notice and you've probably made other plans but my cousin gave me two good tickets for Caulfield and I don't have anyone to go with me.'

'Good tickets for Caulfield Cup Day? Why didn't you say so before? I'd love to go with you, Laura. Just try and keep me away.'

His reaction to the offer was so different from Colin's that she blushed with pleasure. And Declan followed her to her door where he pulled her into his arms and kissed her again. It was only a small kiss, a gentle kiss such as a friend would give, but it made her feel so much better. Her heart was singing again.

5

October, as only the second month of spring in the Southern Hemisphere, offered a remarkable number of changes in the weather. It might be cold and blustery with showers one day and then give a very good imitation of the steaming hot days of summer the next. More often than not, Caulfield Cup Day was a warm herald of the summer to come and today was no exception. Cool at first, the day progressed bright and still with only a few high clouds drifting across the bright blue bowl of the sky.

Laura, for all that she had endured a long diatribe from Eileen concerning the likes of Col Newbold, had slept well and awoken refreshed and ready to enjoy her day at the races. Realizing the weather would be warm, she chose a pretty, flower-printed sundress with a swirling skirt and a matching short-sleeved jacket which she wore with a pair of hot pink sandals and a matching pink straw hat. Declan arrived on the stroke of 10 a.m., looking well scrubbed and surprisingly dashing in a lightweight navy suit.

'You don't have to say anything,' he said in response to Laura's raised eyebrows. 'I don't want to let you down in front of your relatives. I have been to Ascot, you know — I can be as big a suit as the rest of them if I have to.' He twirled Laura to see her new clothes and whistled appreciatively. 'So cute. You look like a schoolgirl today with that hat on the back of your head.'

'That does it!' Laura was young enough not to take such a remark as a compliment. 'I'm changing into my black and white.'

'No time,' he said, catching her hand before she could run away. 'And anyway, I like you just as you are.'

Outside in his car, she found Jodie waiting for them, sprawled across the back seat, dressed in her usual untidy, casual clothes.

'Don't worry.' She grinned at Laura. 'I'm not going to ask you to smuggle me in with the nobs. Just cadging a lift to the track.'

She was as good as her word. Soon as Declan parked the car, she jumped out and left them, putting her fingers in her mouth and giving an ear-piercing whistle to attract the attention of her friends and making Declan wince.

'Ooh, I wish she'd teach me to do that,' Laura said enviously, earning herself a pained look from Declan.

* * *

If Foxie and Daniel were surprised to be introduced to the young Irish horseman instead of the heir to the Newbold millions, they were tactful enough not to say anything.

'I have a feeling we've met before?' Daniel squinted at him, trying to remember.

Declan paused, wondering whether to own up. ''Fraid so,' he said at last. 'I rather rudely interrupted your evening with Laura at the Chinese restaurant.'

'Yes, indeed.' Daniel grinned. 'You took me for an unsuitable suitor.'

'Don't remind me. I felt such a fool when Laura explained. And with your good wife expectin' an' all.'

Laura almost cringed, expecting an outburst from Foxie, who usually resented any mention of her pregnancy, but now she was past the first trimester and beginning to show, she seemed to have mellowed a little and just smiled vaguely, letting it pass.

* * *

'So,' Declan said as he and Daniel propped up the bar between the second and third race while Laura kept Foxie company seated in the stands, 'you have a mare running in race four?'

'Mightie Minnie.' Daniel grinned. 'She was the first of our horses to be owned by a syndicate. Done very well for them, too. Laura tells me you've brought a horse all the way from Ireland to have a go at the Cup?'

'Yeah.' Declan's expression clouded. 'But I have to say it was my uncle's idea, not mine. If I'd had my way, Lance would have stayed right where he was on the Emerald Isle. An' now he's settled so well in Melbourne, I'd almost rather not take him back. I don't hold with the idea of moving horses around, chasing money all over the world.'

Momentarily, Daniel looked surprised as he digested this information. 'But how do you reconcile those views with the job? You're the travelling foreman, aren't you?'

'Also my uncle's idea. He finds me useful enough but we've never really got on. He'll probably give me the sack if Lance doesn't do well in the Cup.'

'I see,' Daniel murmured, feeling sorry for the young man whose future seemed to depend on his uncle's whims. 'And have you decided who's going to take the ride?'

Declan sighed. 'That's a bone of contention between us as well. And time's getting short. Uncle Tavis wants to send out his regular jockey from Ireland but I'd rather see Lance go round with a local man who's familiar with the track.'

'Good decision,' Daniel agreed. 'Can't tell you how many times we've seen overseas jockeys bragging the Cup is as good as theirs, only to come home unplaced.' He produced a card from his wallet and gave it to Declan. 'Simon Grant rides for us quite a lot and I've always been happy with him. He'll listen to what you tell him about the horse and will ride to instructions.'

Declan accepted the card, considering it. 'Look, I don't want to sound ungrateful but surely he'll have a ride in the Cup already, if he's any good?'

'He did have. Unfortunately, the horse broke down in training a few days ago — just cantering, too.' Daniel shrugged. 'It happens. But I'd speak to Simon's agent at once if you want him.'

'Wish I could. But I'll have to check with my uncle first. Nothing makes him more stubborn than if I take a decision without asking him. Maybe I can appeal to the miserly side of his nature — point out how much money he'll save by using a local man.'

'I'll leave it to you, then.' Daniel raised his glass, deciding he liked the straightforward young Irishman, thinking it was a pity Laura couldn't appreciate his sterling qualities. She was so determined to find herself an Australian husband, she couldn't see what was under her very nose.

★ ★ ★

Mighty Minnie looked so good in the mounting yard that by the time Simon Grant was in the saddle and ready to take her out on to the track, she was equal favourite. Once more Laura was left sitting with Foxie while the two men battled the crowds in order to place their bets.

Glancing idly over the throng, Laura spotted Jodie, hanging over the rail at the mounting yard, grinning and waving at Simon Grant. Simon, homely of feature and unused to such attention, was blushing furiously enough to match the dark red of his silks. Quickly, he turned the mare and rode her out on to the track, heading for the starting gates.

Foxie had seen the incident, too. 'Who is that hoydenish girl?' she said. 'I hope she wasn't trying to put Simon off?'

'I don't think so, Foxie.' Laura smothered a smile. 'That's Declan's assistant — Lancelot's strapper. She's probably just a fan.'

'Simon has fans?' Foxie seemed almost startled. Taking her own good looks for granted, she had little empathy for anyone less fortunate.

'Of course he has. There's someone for everyone in this world or — as my mother used to say — a lid for every pot.'

At that moment, the men returned with everyone's betting slips and they settled back in their seats to enjoy the race, smiling at the excited owners of Mighty Minnie, seated in front of them.

The race was short, so in no time at all the wall of horses was thundering towards the final turn, preparing to give their all as they entered the straight. Mighty Minnie, hemmed in behind slower horses, was forced to wait for the field to leave the fence and spread out sufficiently to leave room for her to slip through on the inside. For a moment or two, it looked as if this wouldn't happen but Simon's patience was rewarded as the field drifted off the fence, leaving him the clear run he needed to reach the winning post. Mighty Minnie knew her business and needed no urging. She put her ears back and lifted her speed, overtaking the front runners to win by a clear length to the joy of the crowd, always pleased to cheer in a favourite. Although this race didn't give one of the major prizes of the day, it was a nice win for Mighty Minnie on a prestigious race day and, after the presentation, the whole party celebrated with champagne. Even the scruffy Jodie was allowed to join them. Foxie groaned as the little Irish strapper made a bee-line for Simon Grant although he seemed to enjoy the novelty of receiving so much attention from a girl.

'You absolutely have to let him ride Lance for us in the Cup,' she said as soon as Declan told her of this proposal. 'He'll be so much better than anyone else.'

'Well, I could ride track work for you to start with,' Simon offered. 'See how Lance and I get along?'

'Yes, yes!' Jodie clapped her hands. 'Let's do it.'

'Now, Jodie, don't get ahead of yourself,' Declan warned. 'I'll have to clear it with Tavis first. You know he wants to send out Leo MacCallum.'

'But Leo's so old,' Jodie moaned.

'And still a very good jockey.'

'But Simon is here and he isn't.' She wasn't about to give in. 'And if you tell Mr Martin you've given the job to Simon, he can hardly turn round and back out.'

'Watch him.' Declan's tone was grim. 'But I agree with you — I'd like Simon to take the ride but we'll have to clear it with the old man first.'

★ ★ ★

There were no surprises or upsets in the Caulfield Cup, which was won in style by the horse which had been the clear favourite all day, making the bookies groan. As the shadows lengthened and the afternoon drew to a close, Jodie disappeared to catch up with her friends and Foxie was suppressing yawns, prompting Daniel to suggest he should take her home.

'Sorry to break up the party,' she said. 'But I get really grumpy if I don't get enough rest.'

'Believe it.' Daniel pulled a face, earning himself a good-natured slap from Foxie. 'But you two have the whole of the evening ahead of you. Why don't you go dancing or something?'

'Dancing? After wearing these terrible shoes all day?' Laura held up her high-heeled sandals, dangling from one hand.

'Well, you're not wearing them now, are you?' Daniel teased. 'Little gypsy.'

Laura giggled but refused to be shamed into putting them back on.

Foxie and Daniel left, leaving them to their own devices.

'I'm not that fond of dancing,' Declan confided as they started towards the car park. 'Would you like to take in a movie instead? There's a new *Pirates of the Caribbean* — if you haven't seen it yet?'

'Oh, Declan, that would be such fun. I adore Johnny Depp.'

'Doesn't everyone?' he said, thinking of Lucy, who had been equally enthusiastic over Captain Jack Sparrow. 'It's on at The Rivoli.'

'Where's that? I've heard of it but I'm not sure where it is.'

'Camberwell. It's not far. The screens and the seating are all new but the building itself is old and they've preserved a lot of the original art deco. They have a rooftop bar or we could have a bite to eat in the café before we go in.'

'Both, please. I'm starved. But how come you know so much about Melbourne all of a sudden?'

'John Partridge. He considers it almost a sin to stay in at night. Thanks to him, I've been seeing the sights on a regular basis. We even drove out to Healesville last weekend to see all the native animals.'

'Oh, I love Healesville. Especially all the birds. I'd like to have shown you round there.'

'Really, Laura? Isn't that going to cramp your style when it comes to pursuing your all-important Australian quarry?'

Her expression clouded and he mentally kicked himself, wishing he hadn't made a joke of it.

'You're not going to let me live down Col Newbold, are you? If you must know, it's made me nervous about going out with anyone else.'

'Good. It doesn't hurt to err on the side of caution. Like I told you, these things have to happen naturally.'

'But even nature can do with a shove in the right direction from time to time.'

For this, Declan had no immediate answer and, realizing they would take ages to get to his car while she hobbled on blistered feet, he swept her into his arms and carried her.

'Declan! Put me down. People will think I'm drunk or you're abducting me.' She began to wriggle, trying to break free.

For an answer he merely smiled, held her more firmly and kept walking, carrying her easily as if she weighed nothing at all.

'Declan!' She thumped his shoulder, hating the fact that she was so helpless in his grasp. 'After this, I'm not sure I want to go out with you after all.'

'Suit yourself' He managed to shrug one shoulder. 'I can always go and see Johnny Depp by myself.'

'You will not.'

'OK then,' he said, setting her down beside his car. 'Are you going to be all right in those shoes or do you need to go home to change?'

'No. I can put them on again as soon as my feet have had a rest.'

The cinema was at Camberwell Junction and Laura could see why it was so popular. It combined modern cinema seating and the latest technology with old-fashioned mid-twentieth-century design. All the original art deco features had been retained. Laura could well imagine a time when there was only one large picture theatre on site and people had to queue right around the corner outside those original, chrome-handled doors.

It was busy this night as well, especially for such a popular movie, so they secured their seats before going in search of refreshments. Although Laura enjoyed the ambience of the rooftop bar, it was a cool evening and she wasn't dressed for it in her summer clothes. So they went downstairs again and out on to the street, deciding to eat at a little Italian restaurant Declan had spotted.

'Have what you fancy,' he said. 'They have snacks or more substantial meals, if you're hungry?'

'Pasta would be great,' she said. 'But I'd rather have seafood than meat.'

The waiter arrived and Declan ordered pasta marinara for both of them with a beer for himself and a glass of white wine for Laura. Huge portions arrived promptly and conversation lagged while they gave full attention to the delicious meal. After finishing almost everything on her plate, Laura sat back and blew out a long breath.

'Thanks,' she said, smiling at him. 'That was the best meal I've had in ages. I tend to get a bit grumpy when I'm hungry.'

'Really?' he said, raising one eyebrow. 'I'd never have guessed.'

The film exactly suited their mood, a fun-filled romp which no one was expected to take too seriously. Laura had an infectious giggle which soon spread to the people seated nearby and it seemed that, in no time at all, the film was ending, the credits rolling up the screen.

On the way back to Flemington, Laura talked of how much she had enjoyed the day.

'Thank you, Declan,' she said simply, when he brought the car to a stop outside the apartment she shared with Eileen and the other girls. 'I had a wonderful time.'

'So did I,' he said, sliding his arm along the back of her seat. 'And thank you for introducing me to your cousin and his amazingly beautiful wife.'

'She is, isn't she?' Laura smiled.

'Two redheads.' He considered this for a moment. 'How does that work?'

'Quite well, all things considered. But everyone runs for cover when the sparks start flying.'

Declan nodded. 'I can imagine. But I liked your cousin — good chap. And I hope my uncle will agree to let me book Simon Grant for the Cup.'

'I hope so, too. Seems to me your uncle's a bit of an ogre?'

'No. He's just a vinegary old Irishman who doesn't know when he's well off. He's never been satisfied with anything in his life.'

'Is anyone? Really satisfied with their lot?'

'I am, I suppose.' Declan shrugged. 'And much as I like it here in Australia, I love Ireland more. I like to see real rain and green gardens that can bloom without being watered.'

Laura stifled a yawn. She wasn't in the mood to be reminded of the beauties of Ireland.

'I should go,' he said abruptly. 'It's late, you're tired and I have an early start in the morning. Thanks again for today. It was great.' He removed his arm from the seat behind her without making any attempt to kiss her. Not even a friendly peck on the cheek.

112

She stared at him. Until now, she had been sure he was going to kiss her and was lazily anticipating the pleasure of it. But something had happened to put him off. Somehow, in spite of the relaxed and happy time they had spent together, during the last few moments the barriers had sprung up again and she wasn't sure why. Certainly it couldn't have been anything she said. When she continued to sit there, staring at him wide-eyed, he got out and came round to open the door for her, seeming impatient for her to leave.

'You won't be seeing me for a while,' he said. 'We're less than a month off the big race now and I'll have to concentrate all my energies on Lance. I have to make sure he reaches the peak of his form at just the right time.'

'Yes, I know,' she said, suddenly miserable. 'Oh, Declan, we've had such a lovely day. Please don't spoil it by being so — so . . . ' She felt tears gathering and broke off, biting her lip.

'So what?' He looked back at her, unsmiling. 'You can't spoil something that's come to an end. We had fun today, yes, but it's over. You go back to your life — to continue your search — while I have to get on with mine. G'night, Laura.' And, leaving her standing there on the pavement, he climbed back into the car and drove off without a backward glance.

Laura made her way slowly up the stairs to the apartment, wondering what had upset him. She remembered stifling a yawn when he talked about Ireland but surely it couldn't be something as simple as that?

Upstairs, Jenny, one of her flatmates, was seated at the computer they all shared and which was kept in the 'family room'. She looked up and smiled at Laura. 'I'm all done here. Want to check your e-mails before I sign off?'

'I don't suppose I'll have any — but yes thanks, maybe I will.' Tired as she was, Laura needed something to take her mind off the unsatisfactory parting with Declan.

Jenny disappeared into her bedroom, leaving Laura to type in her password. She had very few e-mails and had almost given up hope of hearing from Bridie but to her surprise and delight, for the first time since they parted, a message was there.

Hello Laura my dear. Her mother's familiar and usual greeting made tears spring to her eyes.

So much to tell and I really don't know where to start or how much time I shall have in this internet café. This is the first moment I've had to myself in weeks and I'm only here because Stan has a toothache. He's gone to the dentist and needs me to drive him home.

Nothing here is as I expected. Here in Florida, Stan is a very different person from the fun-loving man I met in Ireland. He lives not in Miami, as I was led to believe, but some distance away in a decaying mansion which seems to be subsiding into a swamp. They still use oil lamps and a wood burning stove! No electricity — his old auntie won't have it — so no computer or phone.

His Aunt Cassie is over ninety now and a burden to everyone — some days she is more lucid than others — and as for his sister, Fleur, all I can say is that he has a very strange relationship with her. Didn't take long for me to find out I've been brought here to perform the duties of housekeeper rather than wife. No servant will stay once they find out about the lack of facilities. I sleep alone most of the time which suits me just fine. I'd rather not speculate where Stan may be spending his nights.

Laura drew in a sharp breath. From the beginning she had known there was something odd and secretive about Stan. She must find a way to get Bridie away from there!

He doesn't trust me with money now because he received the bill from his credit card shortly after we arrived. Very angry

115

about our little spending spree in London.

Not all that little, Laura reminded herself, thinking of her black and white dress and her mother's designer suit and handbag.

I can't even buy groceries now — he doles out pocket money to me as if I were a child so I'm virtually a prisoner here. How I wish I had listened to you — you always said he was too good to be true, and he was. Oops! Got to go now — I can see Stan coming out of the dentist's looking daggers because I'm not waiting for him in the car. Talk again soon. All love. Mam.

Laura read and re-read the message several times but there was only her mother's e-mail address and no indication at all where the mansion was. Only that it wasn't anywhere near Miami and was subsiding into a swamp.

★ ★ ★

Declan drove slowly back to the motel, wondering how such a perfect day could have ended so badly. Fiercely proud of his homeland, Laura's attitude when he spoke of it touched a nerve. He couldn't understand how she could so readily turn her back on it to live in a crowded metropolis. Maybe he had misread her and she really was a city girl at heart. He sighed, wishing she didn't have

116

such a firm grip on his heart. It would be doubly hard to leave when the time came, knowing how determined she was to stay. He had liked her cousin, Daniel, and was determined to take his advice and engage Simon Grant to ride Lance. If his uncle could see it as a money-saving option, he might stand a chance.

On arriving at the motel, he was relieved to see that John Partridge's car was not in its usual place; he wasn't in the mood for a late night on the town. Briefly, he wondered how John ever got any work done with his horses; he spent more and more time away from them and seemed to be treating this trip as a holiday more than anything else.

He parked his car and moved quietly towards his room. It was nearly midnight and he didn't want to disturb the other guests.

A silver sports car drew up and parked next to his own. He ignored it, continuing on his way until a shriek of familiar laughter made him look back to see that it was Jodie and she was with Simon Grant.

'Oh, Jodie, I don't know,' Simon was saying as she opened the driver's door, urging him to come out. He obeyed her, hesitantly. 'It seems disrespectful to — to sleep with you on a first date.'

'Ooh, Simon, I'll still respect you in the

morning.' She kissed him briefly and giggled. 'And besides, you'll be on the spot to ride track work with Lance.'

'Well, there is that, I suppose,' he said, still looking unsure.

Declan grinned to himself, wondering whether to rescue the young man and deciding against it. Simon was older than Jodie and could surely look out for himself.

'We're going to have Irish whiskey and order a pizza,' she said, smiling mischievously, pushing him towards her door. 'And then we'll have a nice hot shower together while we're waiting for it to arrive.'

Standing in the shadows of his own doorway, Declan realized he shouldn't be listening to this but she was talking in quite a loud voice. It amazed him that for all her untidy clothes and hoydenish ways, his little strapper could be quite aggressively seductive. Suddenly, he wished he had someone to offer him whisky and sex in the shower. But there was only one person with whom he would like to do that and she didn't want him. Tonight she had made that all too clear.

6

'Laura, have you any idea what time it is?' Daniel's sleepy voice answered her almost as soon as the telephone started to ring.

'Oh God, I'm sorry Daniel. It's late, isn't it? Is Foxie — ?'

'Sleeping like a baby. It's OK. You didn't wake her. Wouldn't like to be in your shoes if you did. You do realize that it's after one?'

'Is it? I'm sorry. I'll call back in the morning, shall I?'

'No, I'm wide awake now. But hold on and I'll take this call in the study.'

Laura fidgeted, biting her lips while she waited.

'Now then.' Daniel spoke to her in his normal voice. 'What's the catastrophe that can't wait until morning?'

'It's Bridie. I had an e-mail from her this evening.'

'Well, that's good news, isn't it? You were worried about not hearing from her before.'

'And now I know why. Slavery isn't dead in the Old South yet. Winton's keeping her almost a prisoner over there. She says the house is horrible — way out in the swamps miles from anywhere and with no mod cons — no electricity, not even hot water.'

'Laura, your mother's no fool. She must have had some idea what she was getting herself into with this guy.'

'That's just it. She didn't. He let her think he owned a mansion on the waterfront in Miami. Instead she finds herself living in a crumbling ruin, slowly sinking into a swamp. And he keeps her so short of money, too. She's not even allowed to buy groceries. We have to help her get away.'

'Now slow down a minute. Are you sure this is what she wants?'

'Of course I am. I can print off the e-mail and show you. She even implied that he sleeps with his sister.'

'Now come off it, Laura. You've put two and two together and made five. You've always had a taste for high drama. You shouldn't let that overactive imagination run away with you.'

'Honestly, I'm not.' She was close to tears now. 'But if you can't be bothered to help me — '

'Don't fly off the handle. You know I'll do what I can. But don't forget distance. There's the whole Pacific Ocean between Australia and the States. Short of hiring a bounty hunter or someone to go over and kidnap her,

I don't see what we can do.'

Laura brightened immediately. 'You know of someone? Someone who'd do that?'

'No, Laura, of course I don't. I was making a joke.'

'Well, thanks, Daniel. If you're not going to take it seriously — '

'Lighten up. In the short term, nothing bad is going to happen to your mother — and there's not much we can do now at this time of night. You need to calm down and get some sleep. See how it looks in the morning. Bridie might just be having a bad day.'

'I don't think so. And this is the only e-mail I've had from her. I don't know when she'll get the chance to send me another.'

'Did she leave an address?'

'She didn't have time. Stan was out of the dentist's surgery and she had to, go. How can we find her? There must be miles and miles of the Florida everglades.'

'There are. But if the Wintons are prominent local citizens, known for their eccentricity, they shouldn't be that hard to find. I'll e-mail my connections in the States right now — see what they can turn up.'

'Thank you, Daniel,' she said in a small voice. 'I'm sorry I — '

'Don't be sorry for anything. It's nice that you're so concerned for your mum.'

'I wish we could arrange for her to come here — '

'What? And then I'll have two would-be illegal immigrants on my hands.'

'If I got married, I could sponsor her, couldn't I? She'd be a refugee.'

Daniel swallowed a laugh. 'I don't think an Irish woman, married to an American, would be classified as someone in need of political asylum. Anyway, I was hoping you'd given up on that stupid idea. What about that nice Irish boyfriend of yours? I really liked him.'

'He isn't my boyfriend — or ever likely to be. He says he's too busy with Lancelot's Pride to spend any more time with me.'

'Sounds harsh. But he probably didn't mean it to come out like that. The Melbourne Cup is a big feature race and that's what he's here for, remember. Has to give his horse every chance.'

★　★　★

Laura had no option but to rely on Daniel to carry out his promise to make enquiries about Stanley Winton. Having had the whole of Saturday off to go to the races, she was to take the first shift at the Leprechaun on Sunday morning, always a busy time. People came to socialize or top up their hangovers and many stayed on to have lunch. She looked up hopefully as a group of Irish horsemen came in towards the end of the morning but Declan wasn't among them.

'What's the matter with you, sourpuss?' Eileen peered at her. 'We're supposed to look cheerful, remember? Smiling Irish wenches.' She fluttered her eyelashes and put on a foolish grin until she saw Laura's expression drop even further. 'Oh no, let me guess. You fell out with Declan again, didn't you?'

'Not exactly.' Laura sighed. 'But he says he's too busy working with Lance to spend any more time with me.'

'One date and he dumps you. That's a bit mean.'

'It wasn't really a date, was it? But that isn't why I'm down today. I'm worried sick about my mother — '

'Hey, you two!' Patrick snapped his fingers at them, making them both start. 'You're paid to serve customers, not to stand there chewing the fat over Saturday night.'

Eileen pulled a face at him behind his back and they both went in opposite directions to take more orders, Laura finding herself in the midst of a group of earnest young men who seemed to be tourists.

'An authentic Irish pub.' Their ringleader gazed around, admiring the decor. 'Haven't seen the like since I was in Ireland.'

'And with genuine Irish hospitality!' Patrick broke in, although the young man was speaking to Laura. 'Em here is a native of Ireland herself.' He laid a possessive hand on her shoulder. 'Name your poison an' she'll be happy to serve you.'

Laura gave Patrick a weak smile, wishing he'd go away. She hated it when he tried to take over her customers, playing host. Luckily for her, Eileen had trouble with one of the pumps and Patrick had to go over and deal with it.

'Oh dear.' The young man wrinkled his nose. 'Does he always go on like that?'

'And worse,' Laura giggled. 'Fortunately, he doesn't spend all that much time in the bar. What shall it be, lads?'

'Pot of ordinary VB for all of us.'

'Victoria Bitter?' She gave him a mischievous grin. 'This is an Irish pub, you know. You're supposed to try Guinness.'

The young man lowered his voice. 'To be honest, we don't really like it. Raised on Four X in Queensland.'

'Oh, you're from Queensland,' Laura said, thinking how nice he was. Everything about him was pale brown, his hair, his rather quaint, old-fashioned clothes, reminding her of a bygone era; even his eyes were the colour of sparkling sherry. 'Most people from here go north for their holidays. You're doing it in reverse.'

'Well, we're not exactly on — ' he started to say but Laura wasn't listening, already constructing her own plan. She liked the look of this diffident young man, who seemed as different from Col Newbold as it was possible for anyone to be.

'I could show you around, if you like,' she offered on impulse. 'Take you to the places I love most in Melbourne.'

'All of us?' He glanced at his companions.

'Not really.' She lowered her voice, surprised by her own boldness. 'Just you and me.'

'Ohh.' He went a delicate shade of pink, biting his lip. 'I see.'

'But it's all right if you'd rather not. I don't mind.' She lined the six pots in front of them and noted they all paid separately with handfuls of change, like schoolboys in a sweet shop.

'No, I'd love to do that.' He stayed at the bar to talk to her when the others had left to occupy a table. 'Ms um — Em, isn't it?'

'Actually,' she said, leaning forward to speak very softly. 'My name's Laura. And don't ask why Patrick calls me Em, it's too long a story.'

'A lady of mystery. I like that.' He gave her his special smile that seemed to embrace the world, showing perfect teeth; a smile that made his eyes crinkle with good humour as he clasped her hand, introducing himself 'Celestyn Smith.'

'What a lovely name.' Laura held on, allowing her hand to remain between both of his own. He really was very nice. 'I never met anyone called Celestyn before.'

'Blame my mother.' He grinned ruefully. 'A latter-day hippie.'

If Celestyn's friends didn't care for him to desert them and strike up a friendship with Laura, most of them were tactful enough not to show it. Only one gave her a hard stare as they left, shaking his head in disapproval.

'What's the matter with him?' she asked Celestyn, who had pulled up a stool and was sitting at the bar where he could talk to her.

'Take no notice of George.' He shrugged one shoulder. 'Always thinks he knows how to run everyone else's life.'

'And do you let him run yours?'

Celestyn gave a half-smile as if it wasn't important and looked away.

During the next week, she spent all her free time with her new friend. The only drawback seemed to be that everything had to be done on a shoestring. Celestyn never seemed to have any money and although he wasn't forthcoming about his studies, she concluded he must be a student. Of what, she had yet to discover. She found him both intriguing and exasperating in equal measures. He would go nowhere except on public transport and threw up his hands in horror if she suggested a taxi, even if they were caught in a shower of rain.

If the weather was fine, they walked on the beach or went to a park and spent many hours in the Art Gallery on St Kilda Road. Laura would have liked to see the new Picasso exhibit, on loan from Europe, but Celestyn would visit only that part of the gallery where admission was free. She could only hope his carefulness was due to lack of funds rather than meanness. One day she suggested the zoo but even then he said they should take a picnic.

'The sun is shining,' he said. 'And the forecast is fine.'

'But the wind is still cold and it won't be warm enough to sit outside on a bench and eat sandwiches,' Laura protested.

'I'll bring my thermos then.'

'Celestyn, they have cafés where we can get something hot and warm up.' She was finding it difficult to hide her exasperation.

'And pay through the nose for it.' He

muttered, irritating her further. 'Even the entrance fee is expensive. Maybe we shouldn't go, after all.'

Laura glanced at him, speculating about his mean streak and hoping it wasn't a permanent life stance. Most of the time, he was easy-going and good company. She was beginning to like him a lot and could even imagine being married to him — seeing herself as one of those old-fashioned housewives seen in advertisements, wearing voluminous gingham skirts and starched pinafores, baking cakes for Celestyn and their growing brood. He was kind, safe and seemed to like children; he would be a faithful husband, never giving her cause for grief. Of course, he didn't make her heart thump and her breath catch when he came into the room, not like . . . But she crushed that thought before it could form in her mind. Allow herself to admit she had feelings for Declan and she would be lost. No. With a little more time and encouragement, Celestyn could be 'the one'.

The visit to the zoo was not a success. His thermos of weak instant coffee didn't go far and Laura kept longing for hot chocolate or strong café latte. And he didn't seem very much interested in the animals either. He sighed as he watched the big cats pace up and down their enclosure, looking bored, with nothing to think about but their next meal.

'You have to pity the poor things.' Celestyn gazed at them, shaking his head. 'Prisoners still, even if they're no longer in small cages with bars.'

'Most of these cats are born in captivity,' she said stubbornly. 'They don't know any other life.'

'That's no excuse — they'll have race memory,' he insisted. 'Some part of their brain must remember hot sun and limitless plains. The thrill of hunting and striking down a gazelle and feeling it tremble under their claws, sensing its terror and tasting the hot, sweet blood as it spurts from a mortal wound — '

'Ugh.' She shivered. 'I had no idea you could be so blood-thirsty.'

'It's only nature, Laura. What God put these animals on earth to do. Not to waste their lives, bailed up in captivity for humans to gawp at, and chewing on the bones of dead cows.'

'If that's how you feel, you shouldn't have come,' she snapped, turning away from the lions. 'Let's go and look at something else. The butterfly enclosure is over there. Surely you can't find anything to criticize in that?'

He considered it for a moment. 'Well, most of them aren't native to temperate climes — '

'Oh, for goodness' sake.' Laura left him and stalked ahead, beginning to wonder what she had ever seen in him. And she would throttle Eileen for suggesting the zoo as an ideal place to go on a date. Lots to talk about as well as bushes to hide behind and steal a kiss, she had said. But as yet, Celestyn had attempted no such thing. If Colin Newbold had come on too strongly, she was still waiting for Celestyn to come on at all. Sometimes, she wondered if he even liked her; he seemed so wary of any physical contact. Deciding she had nothing to lose, she tried goading him into action.

'You should hear yourself sometimes, Celestyn. Can't you lighten up and enjoy yourself for once? You do realize we've been dating for almost a month now and haven't even kissed?'

He stopped in his tracks, staring at her as if she'd suggested intercourse, right there on one of the lawns. 'You — you think that's what we're doing? Dating?' he said at last. 'Oh, Laura, no. No. You have it all wrong. You promised to show me your favourite places in Melbourne, that's all.'

'Of course it's not all!' She barely resisted the urge to scream at him. 'What did you think I meant? You speak to me of the nature of big cats. Well, what about human nature?

Hmm? You're a man, aren't you? And I'm a woman although you've scarcely noticed. Isn't it only natural that we should — '

'Stop!' he said, almost in a panic now, holding his hands in front of him as if to ward her off. 'I'm sorry, Laura, if I gave you the wrong impression. But I can't possibly — I could never — '

He backed away a few paces and turned to run, as if he were afraid of what she might do to him if he didn't leave at once.

'Celestyn, what's wrong?' she called after him. 'Can't we talk about it? I'll try to understand.' But she was already losing sight of him as he disappeared into the crowd. She held up his empty thermos, saying in a small voice as she realized he could no long hear her, 'And you left your thermos behind.'

Realizing she was free to please herself, Laura was surprised to feel as if a load had been lifted from her shoulders. To celebrate, she treated herself to hot chocolate together with a huge piece of carrot cake and then she took a taxi home. Unfortunately, Eileen was there and all agog to hear why she was home so early. Exasperated with yet another failure in the marriage stakes, Laura explained the situation as briefly as Eileen would allow.

'You're being too obvious.' Eileen nodded, doing her best to look sage. 'Always makes

131

men nervous. They like to make the running themselves.'

'Make the running?' Laura didn't trouble to conceal her irritation. 'Celestyn doesn't even know how to walk.'

'Nobody's that innocent. Not these days,' Eileen mused. 'Unless of course . . . '

'Unless what?'

'Leave it with me.' She glanced at her watch. 'Saturday night and I have a hot date. Have to go now. But we'll talk again later.'

After Eileen left, Laura checked her e-mails but there was nothing from Bridie and only a brief message from Daniel, whose contacts in the States had little to report. It seemed there were many Wintons residing in Florida and more than one with the given name of Stanley. It would take them a while longer to track down the right one.

Seeing no point in remaining at home alone, she arrived early for the start of her Saturday evening shift. Patrick scowled, glancing at his watch.

'You needn't think I'm paying you overtime,' he grumbled. 'Your shift doesn't start till six and it's only half past five.'

Laura raised her eyes heavenwards, not trusting herself to answer. She knew that if she lost this job, it wouldn't be easy to get another one. Eileen wasn't there either, so she had no chance to discuss Celestyn's odd attitude and behaviour. Half an hour later, when the door swung open to admit Celestyn's friend George, she looked up eagerly, half expecting Celestyn to be with him, full of apologies and even a bunch of flowers. But George was alone and even before she could offer him a drink, he came straight to the point.

'I'm not here to drink, I just wanted a word. Celestyn is very upset.'

'*He's* upset? Well, so am I. You do know he left me flat and I had to make my way home alone?'

'Never mind that. So far as he was concerned, you offered to show him Melbourne. He was shocked when he found out you expected more.'

'Then he's very easily upset,' Laura snapped. 'I asked him why he didn't kiss me. What's so unreasonable about that? It isn't as if I offered to go to bed with him.'

George flinched at her words and she raised her eyebrows and shrugged. Whatever he had to say, she had no intention of making it easy for him.

'Celestyn isn't for you or for any woman. Be very clear on this. You need to leave him alone.'

'Excuse me.' Laura blinked and stifled a giggle. 'Since when is my friendship with Celestyn any business of yours? Oh, unless you and he are — ' And she raised one eyebrow significantly.

'You have a nasty little mind.' George's mouth pursed till it looked like a cat's bottom. 'I warned Celestyn about girls like you. I told him to be careful during this break from our studies — but he's too naïve, too ready to believe the best of anyone. So I made it my business to find out about you. It wasn't hard; you are anything but discreet. And I know you're desperate to find an Australian husband.'

'Oh, hush.' She looked around to see if anyone had overheard. 'You make it sound awful and it's not like that. Not at all.'

'So what is it like, Laura? Celestyn is the best of us and you're putting his very life's work, his vocation, in jeopardy.' George was nothing if not dramatic and people were beginning to stare at him.

'Vocation?' Laura echoed. 'What are you saying? It's a *religious* seminary you attend? That Celestyn — my Celestyn — is going to be a priest?'

George grinned, enjoying her discomfiture. 'Or a monk. At last the penny drops. He was never yours or ever likely to be.'

'But why didn't he have the courage to say so himself?'

'Too soft-hearted. And I daresay he was enjoying the attention you gave him.' George leaned closer. 'He talked of coming to see you to set the record straight. I told him that would be unwise.'

'Why, you — '

'Give him back to us, Laura. Try to see him again and I shall call Immigration and tell them that the Leprechaun should be investigated as a hotbed of illegal immigrants. I'm sure that's the last thing you want.' He gave her an unpleasantly intimate wink. '*Ciao*, baby! Happy Saturday night.'

Laura's cheeks burned with fury and indignation, knowing that there was nothing she could do. She wasn't the only girl who worked here illegally and she wouldn't be responsible for getting anyone else into trouble. Nor did she want a lecture from Daniel, saying *I told you so*. If she were honest with herself, her feelings for Celestyn had never been more than sisterly; no kiss would have ignited the fire that might have grown into passion or love.

Although she continued to smile and serve customers, she was on automatic pilot, lost in her thoughts as she replayed the events of the day. She could only hope George wouldn't be spiteful enough to tip off Immigration anyway.

After a relatively quiet early evening, the pub became crowded and Laura was too busy to think at all. It was one o'clock before the last customer left and she thought of reminding Patrick she should have finished her shift half an hour ago. The kitchen staff were long gone, leaving only Patrick and Laura to turn the last few customers out of the bar. After that, Patrick asked her to balance the till while he went down to check a blocked pipe in the cellar. Then she could go home.

She became so engrossed in what she was doing that she didn't notice the two people sneaking into the bar through the back door which Patrick hadn't yet bothered to lock. Laura didn't see them until they were right beside her when the larger man threatened her with a sawn-off shotgun, making her squeak in fright as she looked up at two faces concealed by black balaclavas, showing only their eyes and mouth.

'No more of that or you'll get a bullet between the eyes.' The man was doing his best to sound tough, although she sensed he was far from confident, sweating and shaking with nerves as he thrust a grey garbage bag into her hands. 'Empty the takings into that and be quick about it. Never mind about the small change.'

'Stop it, Mike,' his companion whimpered, in a voice recognizably female. 'You promised me no one would get hurt.'

'And you can shut up, too!' he said through gritted teeth, turning away from Laura to glare at the girl. 'You said you wanted adventure so don't make me sorry I brought you.'

'I thought it would be exciting,' she wailed. 'But it isn't — it's horrible. I don't want to see anyone hurt.'

While the bandit's attention was diverted by his companion, Laura spied a bag of bread rolls under the counter beside the till. Someone must have put them there, intending to take them home. Without really thinking it through, she shoved them into the bandit's bag, threw a pile of napkins on top of them and knotted it firmly, hoping the man would trust her to have put the money inside.

'All done,' she said, slamming the till shut.

Patrick, arriving from the cellars, saw what was happening and gave a bellow of fear and rage. 'What's happening here? What the hell's going on?'

The bandit, unnerved by the appearance of the landlord, snatched the bag from Laura, took aim and fired a shot over Patrick's head, making him drop to the floor. The noise was deafening in the empty room. Laura also instinctively ducked, terrified that Patrick had been shot.

'Ah, God, you're shooting them!' the girl howled. 'An' you promised me the gun wasn't loaded.'

'And I told you to shut it!' The bandit shoved his whimpering accomplice ahead of him towards the door. 'Get going. We've got what we came for.'

'I don't want any of it. Not any more.' She turned to accuse him. 'You're a murderer!'

'I haven't murdered anyone — but don't tempt me.' He spun her round, prodding her with the gun to urge her on. 'Just move!'

Not unexpectedly, since it was a basic weapon with no safety mechanism, the gun exploded again, right behind the girl. She screamed and fell to the floor, clutching a gaping wound in her buttocks. Within seconds her jeans were soaked in blood.

'Ah, to hell with you, stupid bitch,' the bandit muttered, shaking the bag to reassure himself as he ran for the exit alone. 'Trust you to make a mess of everything. But with this little lot, I can be on a plane in less than an hour.'

As soon as the door slammed behind him, Laura dialled triple 0, summoning both the police and ambulance services. Then she tried to comfort the criminal's accomplice, trying to suppress her horror at the amount of blood still streaming from the wound. Minus the balaclava, she seemed like a schoolgirl, scarcely more than fifteen. Frightened by the sight of so much of her own blood, she was in a state of panic, whimpering in pain and fear.

'It hurts so much.' She clutched Laura's hand. 'Don't let me die, will you?'

'No, no.' Laura tried to sound reassuring. 'It looks bad because there's a lot of blood but it's probably only a flesh wound.' She could only hope she was right. Shattered bones would take much longer to mend.

Half an hour later, the unfortunate girl was on her way to hospital with a police escort, only too willing to tell them everything she knew about her criminal boyfriend.

As the door closed behind them, Patrick slumped at the bar, bewailing his loss.

'Dear God, Laura, the man knew jus' when to strike. He's robbed me of the whole of the weekend's takings.' He leaned there, clasping his head in his hands.

'No, no. The takings are safe and sound, right where you left them. Look.' Laura opened the till to show him.

'But — but how can that be? You gave him the bag with the money. I saw you.'

'Not me. You saw me giving him a sack of old bread rolls an' a bundle of napkins.'

'Girl, you're crazy.' Patrick stared at her in alarm. 'What if he'd checked?'

'Oh, I had a feeling he wouldn't. You could tell they were amateurs. Nervous, too. It was only the gun I was scared of because he was shaking so much.'

Patrick looked at the money lying under the main part of the till and heaved a sigh of relief to find it still there. Then he surprised Laura by grabbing her and doing a wild polka around the room.

'You're a genius!' he crowed. 'Saved my bacon, Laura. I've a big tax bill to pay next week.'

All of a sudden, Laura stopped dancing and stared at him. 'Patrick, you jus' called me Laura.'

'Well, it's your name, isn't it?' He shrugged. 'Maybe I'm not such an' auld fool as you girls like to think. Emerald Green, indeed. As if anyone really has a name like that.'

'So why did you go along with it, calling me Em?'

'Why not? Easier to call everyone Em than remember a string of new names.'

'But you could be investigated. An' then we'd all get into trouble for breaking the law.'

'Well, it hasn't happened yet, has it?' Patrick grinned, putting a finger to his nose. 'Laws are made to be broken, aren't they? I like to think of them as jus' guidelines.'

Laura said nothing. Patrick had not seen the stern expression on the face of the Customs officer, warning her not to outstay her welcome.

7

The following day, the newspapers were full of it and several television news teams had also thought it worth covering the event. Laura would have preferred to forget the whole incident and keep a low profile but that wasn't to be. Because of the two bizarre events — the young girl accidentally shot by her boyfriend together with Laura's courageous deception to save the Leprechaun's takings — someone thought it was newsworthy enough to leak the story to the press. Although Patrick played the innocent, insisting that it was because of the police presence and the ambulance at the scene, everyone knew he would seize any opportunity to gain free publicity for his Irish pub. And there he was, large as life, happily facing the cameras and embroidering the story as he went, exaggerating his Irish brogue.

'When I saw them two an' the gun, I thought we was done for. But our Emerald Green saved the day — she's the real heroine of the hour,' he said, making Laura cringe as she sat at home in front of the television, shaking her head and willing him to be more discreet. 'Who but an Irishwoman would think of such an ingenious ruse?'

Reporters had already been calling her up and hammering at the front door but she remained locked in the apartment, refusing to be interviewed for fear of reprisals. And the last thing she wanted was to come to the notice of Immigration. She had acted very much on the spur of the moment and now reaction and shock were setting in. That man might be well on his way to prison now but for how long? Everyone knew that sentences were generally shorter these days due to overcrowding in gaols. What if he decided to take his revenge on her when he came out? For making a fool of him as much as anything else. Laura sat in her pyjamas and dressing gown, huddled in a blanket, unable to get warm, covering her ears and groaning as there came yet another hammering at the door.

'Go away!' she called, close to tears. 'You're wasting your time. I'm not talking to anyone.'

'Laura! Open up. It's me.'

She gasped, recognizing Declan's voice.

'Oh, Declan, are you alone? Is anyone else out there?'

'Not at the moment. There was a Channel 7 news team but I waited until they'd gone.'

'You're sure they're not round the corner,

waiting to pounce?'

'Stop being paranoid. Jus' let me in before anyone else comes by.'

She opened the door and pulled him inside. He peered at her anxiously.

'You look terrible. Are you OK?'

'Thanks. And of course I'm not OK. I'm scared half to death and Patrick keeps promoting me as some kind of Superwoman. And that isn't funny!' she said in response to his smile.

'I'm not laughing at you, I'm just so relieved you're OK.' He gathered her into his arms and gave her a gentle hug. 'When I heard there had been an attempted robbery at the Leprechaun and a girl had been shot my heart fell to my boots — I was so scared it was going to be you.'

'Were you really?' She looked up at him, basking in his concern.

'You ought not to be by yourself. You've had a shock. I thought at least the altar boy would be here, holding your hand.'

'Not he. I scared him off properly last time. But just a minute.' She narrowed her eyes at him. 'How exactly do you know about that?'

'Oh, your friend Eileen is a mine of useful information and I make it my business to keep up to date with your activities. Anyone could see those lads were straight from the seminary but I reckoned you'd be safe enough with Brother Celestyn while I was so busy with Lance. Wouldn't have had much time to spend rescuing you from the likes of Col Newbold.'

'You've got a nerve, Declan Martin.'

'Don't blame me.' He shrugged. 'If you're stupid enough to take up with a novice priest, who am I to stop you?'

'You might have said something before. I wasted the best part of a month on that man.'

To her increasing fury, Declan laughed. 'Let it go, Laura. Don't you see you can't force the issue like this? You can't make yourself fall in love with someone just because it's convenient. It's not fair to your unfortunate target or to yourself.'

'Since when did you get to be such a wiseacre, Declan Martin? If I want to be psychoanalyzed, I'll hire a professional. I don't need homespun philosophy from the likes of you.'

'Ouch!' He put a hand to his cheek as if she had slapped him. 'But maybe I deserved that.'

She tried to remain stony-faced but a giggle forced its way up, reminding her of their visit to the *Pirates* film and the antics of Captain Jack Sparrow.

'That's better,' he said. 'More like the Laura I know and love.'

'You don't love me. You think more of that lumbering great horse of yours than you do of me.'

'Right now, maybe I do,' he said, examining her more closely. 'I don't suppose you've had anything to eat all day. Otherwise you wouldn't be so irritable.'

Laura realized this was true. There was nothing in the fridge and she had been too scared of running into reporters to risk a quick dash to the supermarket.

'Come on. Get showered and dressed. I'm taking you out to lunch.'

'Declan, I can't go anywhere. Not until all this fuss has died down.'

'Oh yes, you will. You can't hide indoors for ever. We're going to march out of here bold as brass and if anyone tries to stop us, we'll say you're Eileen.'

'But — '

'Come on. It's already after twelve and I'm starved. I've been up since the early hours working the horse.'

'How's he shaping up?'

'Well enough. But we can talk about Lance while we're having lunch.'

Laura left him to read a newspaper while she did as she was told. As she dried her hair later, staring at her solemn reflection in the bathroom mirror, she tried to make sense of the way she felt about Declan. Although he seemed to care about her at the moment, before long he would go back home and forget all about her. He was looking forward to returning to Ireland while she was determined to go on living here. This had always been the main bone of contention between them. Just then he called out, intruding on her thoughts.

'Let's be having you, Laura,' he said. 'We're booked in for lunch at a place in the Dandenongs — they'll keep a table as long as we're there before two.'

'I'm nearly ready,' she called back to him. As she put away the hair dryer, she caught sight of Eileen's new bottle of exotic perfume, perched invitingly on the top shelf in the bathroom cabinet. The carton was a pinkish purple, shading to black, with a woman's naked silhouette etched in silver. Eau de catnip, Eileen had laughingly called it. On impulse, Laura took it out and gave herself a generous squirt in the cleavage. The earlier notes were strong enough to make her cough and she thought of washing it off until Declan called out again.

'Laura!'

'I'm ready!' she called out, running to join him.

As they left the apartment, Laura tensed,

clinging to Declan's hand, but she relaxed when she saw the street was deserted. It seemed that reporters and news teams were just as dedicated to Sunday lunch as everyone else.

On the drive out to the hills, Laura had plenty of time to think of the last time she had come here and of the barbecue party where she had met Colin Newbold. A lot had happened since then. The hills were just as she remembered them, a lush rainforest of tall trees and clean air, with an almost magical atmosphere, cooler and greener than the inner suburbs of Melbourne. Rhododendrons were in full bloom in most people's gardens, making rich splashes of orange and purple between the trees. Declan pointed out the fern trees lining the roads; they were a novelty to him as well. And to their further delight they saw a pair of bright crimson rosellas hanging precariously off one of the fern trees, feasting on the young leaves.

Soon Declan slowed, searching for the place he had been told was nearby. A small notice advertised lunch and afternoon tea, inviting people to take the next turn left. Following this instruction, Declan drove through a pair of open wrought-iron gates and on to a driveway that wound its way higher into the hill. On either side were cultivated gardens; an eclectic mixture of European and Australian native shrubs. Laura wound down the car window to take a better look. Rhododendrons and azaleas were thriving on one side while banksia, grevillea, native fuchsia and many other Australian plants she couldn't identify, occupied garden beds on the other. Small, old-fashioned statues of Grecian ladies stood here and there under the trees, while small fountains and bird baths made a feature of odd corners. Garden seats had been placed under the trees so that visitors could relax and admire the view of the distant suburbs below. The whole place had an atmosphere of peace and tranquillity and Laura was entranced by it.

'Declan, how lovely!' she exclaimed. 'But how could you know it was here? There was only one little notice board down there on the road, offering lunch between twelve and three — '

'And afternoon tea just at weekends,' he finished for her with a smile. 'I wish I could claim the credit but I can't. John Partridge found it. He stopped by for tea one day and took a look at the menu. Told me it would be a nice place to have a Sunday outing and a quiet meal, especially with a girl.'

'It is very romantic, isn't it?' Laura watched a couple strolling in the garden, hand in hand. 'And who would ever know you were here?' She was thinking of how she had suddenly been catapulted into fame and the reporters who might still be lying in wait for her when she got home.

Declan seemed to read her mind. 'Nobody's going to come chasing you here, Laura,' he said, clasping her hand to reassure her.

They parked the car and walked up the wide stone steps to the house. Inside, the décor was that of an old-fashioned country homestead with heavily carved Victorian furniture and stags' heads looking mournfully out from the walls in the hall. Some humorist had decided to use one as a hat stand.

The dining room was a happy mixture of modern lighting and Edwardian elegance, the sideboard heavily carved and with a huge oval mirror, allowing the room to appear twice the size that it was. The tables were set with crystal glasses, more ornate than those common to most commercial establishments, together with heavy, old-fashioned cutlery on starched damask tablecloths with napkins to match.

A smiling waitress ushered them to a table for two in a bay window, overlooking the garden. She promised to return with the menu, saying they could rely on the food being excellent although the choices were few.

'Declan,' Laura leaned across the table to whisper, 'are you quite sure about this? I think it's going to be very expensive.'

'I don't care,' he said, taking her hand. 'It's not every day I get to dine with Patrick's 'heroine of the hour'.'

'Don't.' Her smile faded. 'Please don't remind me of that.'

'Well, I think you deserve a little celebration. I'll bet Patrick didn't offer you anything more than his heartfelt thanks?'

'You're right. He was too busy being relieved that he'd be able to pay his tax bill next week.'

'Are you sure he isn't really a Scot in disguise?'

She laughed. 'No. He makes a profession of being an Irishman. But he pays the staff as little as he can get away with and he's more careful than most.'

'Perhaps he's related to my Uncle Tavis,' he said with a wry smile, accepting the menu from the waitress. Laura was right. The price of food here was certainly top of the range. 'Now what would you like?' he said, resigned to the fact that his credit card was going to take a hammering. 'Since we're here, we should make the most of it and have all three courses. Start with the oysters mornay, have the traditional roast beef mains — can't resist

151

Yorkshire pudding — and then see if we have room for dessert?'

'Sounds good to me.' Laura sat back and smiled at him. 'Thank you, Declan. I feel better already.'

They ordered mineral water and a bottle of the local Merlot to have with their main meal. The oysters came and were quickly despatched, somehow making them feel more hungry than ever. And when the main course arrived, they saw it had been cooked to perfection, accompanied by crisp roast potatoes, young carrots and tender, flat green beans. The Yorkshire pudding was light as a soufflé and the whole platter looked as if it had been lovingly prepared by somebody's mother rather than a chef in a restaurant kitchen. They ate in companionable silence, both too hungry to offer more than sighs of pleasure over the delicious meal.

'Now . . . ' Declan grinned at her after their empty plates had been cleared away. 'Can you be tempted by the chef's special chocolate mousse with raspberries or would you prefer the pineapple upside-down cake?'

'I shouldn't eat anything more at all,' Laura said. 'But greed could take me there. Chocolate mousse sounds far too good to miss.'

And it was. The lightest possible mousse,

served with raspberries and a large dollop of cream.

By the time coffee arrived, together with chocolate mints, they were both replete. Laura sighed and sat back, smiling at her companion across the table.

'Thank you, Declan,' she said. 'How did you know so exactly what I would like?'

He shrugged. 'I just gave you what *I* would like, that's all. We're not so different, you know. Maybe we're meant to be soul mates but you can't see it yet.'

'But soul mates are for life.' Laura sat up straighter, wondering where the conversation was leading. 'I can't get too close to you because soon you'll go back to Ireland and leave me behind.'

'Well, that's your choice, isn't it?' he said softly. 'Not mine.'

'No, Declan,' she whispered. 'Don't go there. Not now. I don't want to argue with you and spoil such a perfect day.'

He shrugged and gave yet another wry smile. They finished their coffee, Declan paid for the meal, and they went outside to join others strolling in the gardens. The wind had dropped and the day was surprisingly warm. The grounds of the mansion seemed to spread over several acres, wide green lawns sloping down on one side of the house and a labyrinth of secluded gardens on the other, each with a characteristic of its own. They followed a gravel path alongside a small box hedge and Laura cried out in delight at what she saw.

'A wishing well!' She started running towards it. 'I haven't seen one since I left Ireland. Quick — we both have to make a wish.' She kneeled at the edge of the pool and fished in her purse to pull out a shiny new dollar. A notice informed them that it would eventually find its way to a local charity. Closing her eyes, she took a deep breath, holding it while she tossed her coin into the well and made her wish. 'Now you,' she smiled at him, opening her eyes again.

'You take this seriously, don't you? What did you wish for?'

'I can't tell you or it won't come true,' she teased. 'But I know exactly what you're going to wish for.'

'Oh, do you?'

'Yes. You'll wish for Lance to take home the Melbourne Cup.'

'Very nice. But that's rather up to Lance, isn't it? And Simon, of course.'

Nevertheless, he found a coin and flipped it, making it spin furiously before it landed in the water almost on top of Laura's.

'So your uncle agreed that Simon could take the ride?'

'Only after a lot of fast talking on my part. And he'll blame me if we don't come home with a prize.'

'That's not fair.'

'My Uncle Tavis doesn't know the meaning of 'fair'.'

'And have you been keeping an eye on the competition? What are Lancelot's chances — realistically?'

'Who knows? He travelled without losing too much weight and settled in well. He's bonded with Simon, he's fit enough and of course Jodie spoils him outrageously, hand feeding him and generally treating him like a prince. An exceptional overseas horse is capable of winning here but the local trainers are always anxious to keep the Melbourne Cup on home ground.'

'But they do want overseas competitors, don't they? To make the Cup an international event?'

'The organizers and racing clubs do, of course. But I was talking to John Partridge along these same lines and we both reached the same conclusion. On the one hand, they need the visitors and the worldwide interest that comes with them but at the same time most Australians want to see the race won by a local champion. I've done the best I can with Lancelot's Pride. He's ready but he hasn't peaked and I hope he'll be on top of his form on the day. That's really all I can do.'

'Good. I'll certainly put a few dollars on him and cheer him on.'

'Talking of which, the big day is just over a week away now. Would you like to accompany me as my guest?'

'Yes, please. I thought you'd never ask.'

'Well, you've been a bit busy, haven't you? What with the millionaire's son and the altar boy — '

'Poor Celestyn. You shouldn't call him that.'

'And you should've known better than to date someone with a name like Celestyn.'

'I liked his name,' she said defensively. 'And after that bad experience with Colin, I needed someone entirely different.'

'He was that all right. And while you were busy with them, you were totally ignoring the home-grown product — me.' And before she realized what he would do, he leaned forward and kissed her, gently but firmly, on the lips. As she didn't pull away immediately, he started to deepen the kiss until he realized she was staring at him with an odd expression in her wide open eyes.

'What's wrong now?' he murmured,

releasing her for a moment. 'Don't tell me you didn't like it? I'm not a complete fool, you know. I can tell whether or not a girl likes being kissed.'

'Of course I liked it. I like you. But I can't go falling in love with you, Declan.'

He placed a finger under her chin and lifted it, forcing her to look him in the eye. 'Isn't it a bit late to say something like that?'

She pulled away from him and stood up, folding her arms and hunching herself against the cold. The sun had already disappeared behind gathering clouds and she was suddenly chilled. Declan took off his jacket and draped it around her shoulders.

'We should go,' he said, striding away towards the road which would take him to the car park.

'Declan, wait,' she called after him. 'I owe you an explanation at least.'

'You don't owe me anything, Laura.' He turned to look at her, sounding tired and dispirited. 'It's not your fault. I was hoping for something different, that's all.'

'Please try to understand. This isn't about you or me — '

'No, it isn't, is it,' he snapped back at her. 'It's about an image, a dream you carry in your mind of this perfect man you have yet to meet. Or maybe he doesn't have to be perfect

— just able to make you an Australian citizen. Well, I'm tired of playing second fiddle to him.'

'Wait. You can't just go off and leave me here.'

'No? Watch me.' He kept on walking, only to stop and scowl as he heard her giggle. 'All right, what is it now?'

'Your car keys and your wallet are in this jacket. I could throw them in the wishing well.'

'You wouldn't.'

'No?' she said, imitating his earlier tone. 'Watch me.'

Realizing he had quickened his pace to catch up with her, she squealed and ran back towards the wishing well. Exhilarated and half frightened at what he would do, she was too breathless to run fast. He caught up with her easily and spun her to face him.

'And what is that wonderful perfume?' he demanded of her. 'It's been driving me crazy all day.'

She gasped as she realized he was staring at her with an expression containing both rage and lust. Not a good combination. Too late, she realized it had been a mistake to spray herself so liberally with Eileen's new perfume.

Before she had time to protest or laugh him out of it, he started kissing her fiercely and with no gentleness at all. His afternoon stubble scraped her chin as he took possession of her mouth, giving her no time to breathe. His breath was sweet, tasting of coffee and mint, and he looked as if he was about to devour her whole. He almost ripped his jacket from her shoulders and threw it to the ground and she tensed, half expecting him to throw her on top of it. He was holding her so close, she could feel his heart beating furiously against her breast as her own heart began pounding in response. He paused only to start unfastening the tiny buttons of her blouse.

'Declan, please,' she whispered. 'We're not alone here. Someone might come.'

'Then they can go away again, can't they?' he muttered. Acting as if he scarcely knew what he was doing, he made a love-bite on her neck before moving lower to make another on the curve of her breast. Feeling the blood rush to her face, which was burning with excitement and humiliation, she moaned half in pain, half in pleasure as he made these marks of ownership, knowing she would bear them for some time. He drew her closer, pressing her body against him so she could feel his erection even through his clothes and her own.

Oh dear, she thought, almost detached for

a moment, *I'm going to lose my virginity right here in this garden and in full public view*. And what was even more odd was that she didn't care. Clinging to Declan's shoulders for support, she gave herself up to the pleasure of his lovemaking and succumbed to the feeling of melting inside. He smelled wonderful, too, of male musk with just the faintest hint of straw and stables. If this was what it felt like to give herself to a man, she was ready. More than ready.

Suddenly, she realized he had stopped kissing her. His arms still held her, offering support, otherwise she would have collapsed to the ground.

'Laura, I'm so sorry,' he whispered. 'I don't know what came over me.' He winced, tracing the outline of the love-bite on her throat.

'Well, it came over me, too,' She said shakily, trying to lighten the mood and bring them both down to earth again. 'But I'd better warn Eileen to be careful with that new perfume.'

He picked up his jacket and slung it around her shoulders again, wincing and turning up the collar to hide the mark he had made.

'That bad, huh?' Laura reflected his expression. 'I should've mentioned that I bruise easily.'

'Your skin is all too delicious,' he

murmured, reaching for her again. 'And what is that perfume? I'll buy you some.'

'I don't know. Bound to be something provocative.' She smiled mischievously, keeping herself out of reach. 'But I don't want any. I'm through with testing your self-control.'

'Spoilsport,' he said without rancour, catching up with her as she strode purposefully towards the car park.

8

The first Tuesday in November lived up to its reputation of being changeable. Although the early part of the day appeared to be bright and warm, the forecast predicted that after midday the weather would deteriorate into squalls and heavy showers. Certainly not the weather for the light summer shift and straw hat Laura had set her heart on wearing. Seeing the battery on her mobile was low, she put it aside in order to recharge and called Foxie for advice on the landline.

'In these conditions, I wouldn't go at all,' her cousin's wife said. 'Flemington can be draughty at the best of times and I've seen many a good umbrella turned inside out by the wind. You'll get blown off your feet today if not soaked to the skin. Daniel has to be there, of course — we have a runner in one of the early races — but I'm giving it a miss this year.'

Laura knew that this wasn't the whole story. Foxie, initially far from pleased to find herself pregnant with twins, had recently had a complete change of heart when it seemed as if she might lose them. That crisis had been averted but she had been warned to rest and not overexert herself. Laura knew this was difficult for Foxie who had always been very active and liked to be fully involved in the day-to-day work of their racing stables.

'I need you to help me decide what to wear,' Laura said, taking another look into her wardrobe that contained nothing suitable for such an occasion. 'Because Declan has invited me to go as his guest.'

'Oh, has he?' Foxie seemed to find this amusing. 'Interesting.'

'Well, don't build too much into it. We're just — '

'Good friends.' Foxie finished the sentence for her. 'Yeah, yeah. I know. So you need something a bit more special than if you're just mingling with the crowd.' Foxie paused, thinking for a moment. 'What about that nice little number you brought from London?'

'Declan's seen it.'

'So what? Men don't remember clothes.' Foxie giggled. 'Not unless they're wantonly revealing.'

Laura examined the dress although she had already decided against it. 'My mother wouldn't have bought it for me if it was. Anyway, the label says dry clean only. I can't risk getting it wet — it might shrink.'

'He'd certainly remember it then. Look, if you've time to come over here, you can have something of mine.' Foxie sighed. 'I'm the size of a house now and I'm never going to fit into these clothes again.'

'I'm sure you will. But I'll take you up on the offer and borrow something.'

'Good. And if you can get here and choose something quickly, Daniel says you can catch a ride to the course with him.'

'You're on. Haven't heard from Declan. Far as I know, he's travelling in with the horse.'

Laura flagged down a taxi and was at Daniel's house in less than fifteen minutes. Although she could have spent many happy hours looking through the clothes in Foxie's enormous walk-in wardrobe, time was short and she knew Daniel would go without her if she took too long. She tried on several dresses but settled on a comfortable, figure-flattering jersey the colour of violets that Foxie assured her could withstand a brief shower. Foxie also insisted on giving her a glamorous black jacket made of something resembling watered taffeta but was in fact waterproof.

'Keep them and with my blessing,' Foxie said in response to her grateful hug. 'I've always thought violet a bit of a cliché with red hair and that dress looks wonderful on you, it brings out the colour of your eyes. You'll knock him cold.'

'I don't want to. As I told you we're — '

'Just good friends.' Foxie grinned, finishing the sentence for her yet again.

Daniel glanced into the room, tapping his watch. 'Sorry to break up the party, girls, but we need to get going. Oh, wow!' he said, catching sight of Laura.

'Wow, indeed.' Foxie gave a wry smile. 'You never said 'wow' to me when I wore that.'

'Oh but, darling, I didn't mean — '

'Only kidding.' Foxie gave him a friendly punch on the shoulder. 'But she does look wonderful, doesn't she? Now what else does she need? A good handbag.' She turned back to Laura, plucking her well-worn bag off her shoulder. 'You can't carry that awful satchel thing, it'll ruin the whole effect. What about this?' She picked up a shiny black bag with a golden chain and a fancy clasp.

'Foxie, I can't.' Laura's eyes widened. 'That's Chanel, isn't it?'

'Probably only a knock-off' Foxie shrugged. 'Take it. I'm about to have twins, remember? I'll need a handbag big enough to hold nappies and hang on the back of a pusher.'

'Foxie, please.' Daniel broke in yet again. 'Can we go now?'

'A big handbag just encourages a girl to fill it with junk,' Foxie said, ignoring him. Quickly, she transferred Laura's wallet and a few other items from the satchel into the more compact Chanel. 'You can pick this up again later.' Foxie nodded, finally satisfied with her transformation of Laura. 'No point in taking a hat — you'll spend all day trying to hold on to it.'

★ ★ ★

On the way to the racecourse, the roads were unusually crowded because it was Cup Day. Daniel could only fume as they had to wait longer than usual to pass through dozens of traffic lights on the way. By the time they reached Flemington it was almost eleven, with just over half an hour to spare until Foxie's Fancy was due to race.

'Sorry, Laura, I'll have to dash,' he said, locking the car. 'Need to catch up with the owners — they'll be wondering where I am.' And, without waiting for her reply, he was gone.

Alone, Laura realized that although she had been admitted to the exclusive car park with Daniel, she had no ticket or means of identification to get inside the owners' and trainers' enclosure. Concentrating on her search for something to wear, she had quite forgotten to firm up arrangements with Declan. Too late, she remembered her mobile — useless now because it was at home waiting to be charged. She chewed her lip, wondering what to do.

'Laura, hi!' She heard a girl calling her. 'There you are.'

With a measure of relief, she recognized Jodie, Lancelot's strapper, walking towards her with Simon Grant.

'Declan's been looking for you,' the girl told her. 'When he couldn't raise you on the phone, he went round to your flat to collect you and you weren't there — '

'Oh, no.' Laura winced. 'We didn't make firm arrangements. I assumed we were going to meet here.'

'He's pretty upset. He thought you'd forgotten and gone off somewhere else.'

'No! How could I forget Melbourne Cup Day? My cousin's wife was finding me something to wear.'

'And well worth the finding.' Simon eyed her in the designer dress, earning himself a jab in the ribs from the girl beside him.

'I should get back to Lance,' Jodie said. 'He's pretty keyed up today and if I'm not there, he might get overexcited.' She pushed a strand of hair back from her face, allowing

167

Laura to catch sight of a solitary diamond winking on the third finger of her left hand.

'Hey, wait a minute,' Laura said. 'That's not an engagement ring?'

'Certainly is.' It was Simon who replied. 'Jodie agreed to marry me just last night.'

'It's lovely,' Laura murmured, admiring the stone on Jodie's red-knuckled, work-worn little hand. At the same time she felt a pang of envy that the other Irish girl should have succeeded where she had so spectacularly failed. 'Congratulations. You'll be staying here in Australia, then? What does Declan think about that?'

'Oh, I won't be living here. I couldn't leave Lance.' Jodie put an arm around her fiancé and hugged him. 'But there are plenty of opportunities for jockeys on our side of the world. Simon's thinking of moving to Ireland.'

This latest news left Laura speechless for a moment. At last she drew a deep breath and said, 'Would you mind telling Declan I'm here? I haven't a ticket, you see, or any sort of a pass — '

'Ooh, sorry, I should've thought.' Jodie kissed Simon briefly and gave him a little shove. 'Be seein' you later, love. Good luck in the big one. I know you'll be doin' your best for Lance.'

'He'll be the least of my worries. He's a beautiful horse.'

Laura remained near the entrance, feeling conspicuous, as Jodie vanished inside. Keeping an eye on her, the doorkeepers exchanged knowing glances, taking her to be one of those girls who haunted the major race meetings, trying to get into privileged areas without a pass. This was embarrassing. What should she do if Declan had taken the huff and decided to leave her outside?

★　★　★

Inside, Jodie was hunting through the crowd, looking for Declan when he spotted her first.

'Jodie, what the hell are you doing up here?' he snapped. 'Why aren't you with Lance?'

'I was on my way back to him now,' she said, taken aback that the usually easy-going Declan should speak so sharply. 'But don't worry, I'm sure he's OK. A friend of Simon's is with him — he's very responsible — and the place is swarming with security, anyway.'

'Some of whom might not be what they seem. There's a rumour going around that someone's been trying to get at some of the Cup runners — '

'To harm them? Poison them?' Jodie felt

colour draining from her face.

'No, nothing as serious as that. They're saying a 'milk-shake' or something just enough to disqualify them — bi-carb.'

'Then what are we waiting for?' Jodie quickened her pace. 'Lets get back to him now.'

Chastened by Declan's unaccustomed severity and full of concern for Lance, Jodie completely forgot to tell him that Laura was waiting outside, unable to get in without a pass.

★ ★ ★

Some time later, Laura grew anxious, beginning to pace up and down. A group of people, laughing in anticipation and dressed smartly enough to be joining the Queen at Ascot, crowded towards the entrance. For a moment, she considered trying to sneak in behind them until she saw that the doormen were meticulously checking and counting every pass. She had made a genuine mistake in her arrangements with Declan and she could only hope he would be generous enough not to hold it against her. But as time wore on and as the hands of her watch crept slowly towards the half hour, she could only conclude he had taken petty revenge. She went to the window and peered in, hoping to catch sight of her cousin, but he was nowhere to be seen. This achieved nothing more than further smirks from the people guarding the entrance to this exclusive enclosure.

Dispirited, she turned away. She hadn't even been able to see Daniel's horse, Foxie's Fancy, although she heard the race through the loudspeakers and already knew that his promising filly had won. Of course — that was why she couldn't see him. He would be downstairs accepting the prizes with the syndicate owning the horse.

'Hey, there! Laura, isn't it? Laura Flanagan!'

Staring at the ground and lost in the gloom of her thoughts, she was startled to hear someone calling her. She looked over her shoulder, not entirely pleased to see that it was Colin Newbold striding towards her, dressed to kill in a new grey suit with a fancy embroidered waistcoat and a yellow rose in his buttonhole. It wouldn't have surprised her to see him wearing a top hat.

'It is you, isn't it? And looking wonderful, too.' He glanced appreciatively at her borrowed clothes. 'But you're not leaving already? It's scarcely midday and you can't leave before seeing the Cup.'

'Oh, well.' She swallowed the lump in her

171

throat, blinking away incipient tears. 'I was supposed to meet someone and they — they — '

'Didn't turn up? Well, more fool them.' He turned to the beautifully made-up blonde standing just a few paces away with her arms folded, watching them, her expression dark with disapproval. 'You don't mind if Laura joins us, do you, darling?' And without waiting for the girl's response, he seized Laura by the arm, steering her towards the Members' Enclosure, introducing them as he went. 'Laura, this is Jill Westacott.'

'His long-suffering fiancée,' the girl broke in with a tight little smile. She had a low and pleasing voice which was at odds with her disagreeable expression.

'I'm all right on my own, really.' Laura pulled herself free. 'I wouldn't want to intrude.'

'Nonsense.' Colin caught her again, putting his other arm around his fiancée and drawing her close to make an uncomfortable three-some. 'We always have time for friends on Melbourne Cup Day, don't we, Jilly? And I won't take no for an answer. You're coming with us.'

'Hurry up, then.' The girl glanced at her race programme and then at the oversized diver's watch on her wrist. 'My dad has a horse running in the last race before the Cup and I don't want to miss it.'

'That's hours away,' Colin argued.

As they entered the most exclusive area of the racecourse, one of the doormen pointed out that Colin's pass was for himself and one other guest, not two. Colin sighed meaningfully and a fifty-dollar note changed hands to settle the matter as Jill, huffing with impatience, stalked in ahead of them. Colin seemed to be enjoying the situation, oblivious to the fact that the situation was awkward for both girls. Or was he? Briefly, Laura wondered which of them he was trying to punish by forcing them into each other's company.

'We'll have champagne all round to get the ball rolling,' Colin led them towards the bar that seemed to be doing good business already. To Laura's relief, he didn't leave her alone to make conversation with Jill while he bought the drinks but found seats for all three of them at the bar.

'Now . . .' Jill took the opportunity to look Laura up and down, making her even more happy that she had borrowed Foxie's expensive designer clothes. 'How come you know Colin? And do I detect a bit of an Irish brogue?'

'If you must know, she's a friend of

Eileen's.' Colin answered the question for her. 'They work at that Irish pub near the racecourse — '

'Oh, the Leprechaun.' Jill brought as much scorn into her voice as she could muster. 'Can't stand it there. It's always so crowded.'

'Yes, it's quite popular,' Laura observed.

'And wasn't there some trouble recently?' Jill fixed her with an eagle's gaze. 'I hope you're not the idiot who stood up to those bandits? Damned if I'd risk getting killed for my boss's money.'

'Jilly, you don't have a boss,' Colin reminded her. 'And you've never done a stroke of work in your life. Stop trying to push Laura's buttons.'

'I want to see what she's made of, that's all.' Jilly's smile was mean. 'If you can't stand the heat, stay out of my kitchen.'

'Look, I really think I should go.' Laura wriggled off her bar stool, anxious to leave. She was feeling more and more uncomfortable with these two who bickered and fought like an old married couple. They seemed to thrive on goading each other and making contentious remarks.

'Not before you've had a glass of champagne.' By now, Colin had hold of a bottle of vintage Moët and was already filling three glasses.

Meaning to drink just one glass and make herself scarce, Laura took a sip and almost sneezed as the bubbles went up her nose.

'Well, I'm interested in the racing, even if you're not.' Jill drank half a glass of champagne and slid off her stool, her long legs allowing her to do this more elegantly than Laura. She snapped her fingers at Colin. 'Let's have some money, Col. Dad gave me some tips for the next race.'

'Which I suppose you're not sharing with us?' Colin said, parting with three fifty-dollar notes. Sighing, Jill continued to snap her fingers until he gave her one more. Clearly, Ms Westacott didn't wager in fives and tens. Without thanking him, she disappeared into the crowd waiting to place their bets.

With her safely out of sight, Colin turned the full force of his charm on Laura. 'I owe you an apology, Laura. I'm so sorry about that other night. I behaved like an idiot, a complete boor. I'd like to make it up to you, if you'll let me.'

Laura stared at him, exasperated. 'Colin, you have a fiancée who's right here with us in this room. There isn't any place for me in your life.'

'Why ever not?' He seemed genuinely surprised.

'Because I'm not in the habit of stealing

men from other girls.'

He laughed as if she'd made a particularly funny joke. 'Have you any idea how old-fashioned and prissy that sounds? It's OK. Jilly understands. She has her own agenda. We have what you might call an 'open' engagement.'

'Really? And does that mean you'll be having an 'open' marriage as well?'

'Very likely.'

'Well, just so you know, I've no intention of being anyone's little bit on the side.' And, without thinking what she was doing, Laura picked up her glass and swallowed her champagne as if it were lemonade, intending that to be her parting shot. On an empty stomach, it went straight to her head. Quickly, Colin refilled it. She could have left it standing there but, to give herself Dutch courage, she drank most of that as well. She opened her mouth to say a firm goodbye but instead of words she gave a resounding, unladylike belch. This broke the tension immediately, making them both laugh.

'That's better.' Colin smiled wolfishly. 'Now you're starting to relax and enjoy yourself. And, pardon me for mentioning it, but have you met any vampires lately? That's a savage-looking bite you have there on your throat.'

'Oh!' Laura's hand flew to hide it. In her haste this morning, she had forgotten to cover it with concealer.

'Oh, indeed.' Colin smiled directly into her eyes. 'Maybe you're not so much of a convent girl after all.'

Jilly returned and lowered her sun-specs to peer disapprovingly at Laura, who was now pink in the face, flushed with both alcohol and embarrassment.

'Oh dear, Colin,' she murmured. 'Tut. I leave you alone for five minutes and you're filling her up with champagne, getting her drunk. It won't get you anywhere, though. She'll only get sick and you'll have to send her home in a taxi.'

'You know, Jilly.' He sat back, regarding her. 'You really are a twenty-four-carat bitch.'

'Darling, I know.' She blew him a kiss, laughing genuinely for the first time and irritating him further by leaning forward to pat his cheek. 'That's why you love me so much.'

Muttering an excuse about finding the ladies' room, Laura finally made her escape. She couldn't spend another moment in the poisonous atmosphere surrounding that couple, whose one aim in life seemed to be scoring points and ruining the day for each other.

In the ladies' room, she splashed cold water in her face in the hope of bringing down the colour. Having seen more than enough of Melbourne Cup Day already, she decided to find another way out and go home.

On the way, she bumped into Daniel. 'Congratulations!' She gave him a hug. 'I heard Foxie's Fancy win.' Quickly, she told him about the misunderstanding with Declan and how she had managed to get inside after all.

'Haven't been drinking, have you?' He noted her shiny, red cheeks and over-bright eyes. 'You know it always goes straight to your head. And what have you done to Declan? He reckons you stood him up.'

'The other way round, I'd say. I saw Jodie, his strapper, and asked her to let him know I was stuck outside and couldn't get in without a pass. I waited over half an hour and he didn't come. He just left me standing there.'

'Probably not his fault. There was a scare down at the stables — a rumour of an intruder all set to cause mischief with some of the Cup runners. Luckily, that's all it turned out to be — just a rumour. But it gave him a few nasty moments. Jodie, too.'

'Well, he could have explained it later.'

'How? When you'd gone off with your mates to guzzle champagne?'

Before Laura could answer this accusation, Declan himself loomed before them, hands on hips, one eyebrow raised, his expression cool.

'So you've finally torn yourself away from Col Newbold? I saw you in there, giggling with him and drinking champagne.'

'So why didn't you come over and rescue me?'

'You didn't look as if you needed it. Besides, I've picked up the pieces behind him already. Maybe I didn't feel like doing it again.'

'Look, I have to go,' Daniel said, not wanting to buy into what looked like developing into an argument. 'Things to do — people to see.' He disappeared into the crowd while Laura and Declan didn't stop glaring at each other long enough to register that he was no longer there.

'That's so unfair.' Laura was starting to lose it, her temper rising. 'Jodie promised to tell you I was outside. I stood there for half an hour and you never came.'

'So you took up with Col Newbold again instead.'

'I didn't take up with anyone. His fiancée was there.'

'Not when I saw you.'

'Well, she was there for most of the time. I

179

don't think she trusts Col on his own.'

'Sensible girl. But why aren't you answering your mobile?'

'Because I don't have it. It needed recharging and I left it at home,' Laura wailed.

All of a sudden his mood changed; he relaxed and began to smile. 'What a catalogue of disaster. One misunderstanding after another. Perhaps we should draw a line under what's happened and start the day all over again.'

'If it isn't too late,' She said, tears threatening again.

'Of course not. And don't cry. You look amazing today — like a princess — and Irish princesses never cry.' He leaned forward and kissed her trembling lips as a tear spilled over and rolled down her cheek. He took out a clean white handkerchief and wiped it away. She took it from him and noisily blew her nose. 'Keep it,' he said with a wry smile. 'Now, I don't know about you but I could do with some lunch inside me before the big race.'

'Really? In your shoes, I'd be too nervous to eat a thing.'

'Oh, this isn't the first time I've trained up a horse for a major race. No point in getting the collywobbles now. I've bought a pile of sandwiches I was taking to Jodie. Care to join us?'

'Yes, please.' She said in a small voice, following him down to the stalls where the runners for the Cup had been housed.

As soon as she saw Laura, Jodie clapped her hands to her mouth.

'I'm so sorry!' she said. 'I was so worried about Lance that I forgot all about you.'

'That's OK.' Now that the misunderstanding was cleared up, Laura was prepared to be gracious. 'Can we break out those sandwiches — I'm starved.'

Although the weather had been fine during the early part of the day, storm clouds were gathering until the sky became the colour of an angry bruise. Although it wasn't yet raining, the wind howled across the course, tearing off picture hats and sending them bowling across the lawns, making their owners run screaming after them. Not satisfied with causing this mayhem, the wind plucked at the light summer dresses, raising skirts waist high and embarrassing those girls who had tempted fate by wearing such flimsy clothes.

And then, just half an hour before the running of the Cup, the rain came down in huge drops, adding to the misery of the wind-blown crowd. Those with umbrellas tried to raise them but they were quickly snatched from their grasp or turned inside out. It wouldn't be the first time but it looked as if the Cup was to be run in torrential rain. Declan grinned, rubbing his hands.

'Bring it on,' he said. 'The more it rains, the softer the ground and the better Lance is going to like it.'

'I hope you're right,' Jodie said. 'But it's going to be slippery out there.' She was thinking of Simon. Unsmiling, she fastened a hooded raincoat under the bib, bearing the prestigious number — One — that Lance would wear as the visiting Irish champion and therefore carrying top weight. Fortunately, he had drawn barrier Ten, giving him one of the best possible chances in the race, in spite of his handicap. With a last pat of Lance and a thumbs up to Jodie, Declan and Laura moved off, braving the storm once again on their way to the stands.

Laura buttoned down Foxie's rain jacket, protecting the Chanel purse inside, relieved that she didn't have to worry about losing a hat although her hair was dripping wet in a matter of seconds.

In the stands, people were friendly, greeting Declan and wishing him well, shaking him by the hand. Although he knew their allegiance was really to other horses, these Australian owners and trainers were courteous, kind and generous in their good wishes. Only John Partridge was less than affable, faced with the high expectations of his horses' owners, who had descended on Melbourne in force a couple of days ago and were now behaving as if the Cup were already theirs.

'Didn't your people turn up, then?' John glanced at Laura, who resembled a mermaid with the rain making her abundant hair spring into curl. 'That's a shame. Not enough faith in the old fella, eh?' He smirked. 'Best of luck, then, Declan. You're going to need it in this weather with Lance carrying top weight.'

'Oh, I dunno.' Declan allowed his Irish accent to become more pronounced than ever. 'Lance isn't averse to a drop o' the Lord's good rain. I'd say you'll be needin' the luck yourself with that lot in tow.'

'Don't I know it.' John smiled ruefully, dropping his truculent attitude. 'If we don't scrape into a place, there'll be hell to pay.'

'Best of luck to both of us, then.' Declan escorted Laura to their seats. She was shivering with both excitement and anticipation and wondered if Declan felt the same. He surprised her by seeming unusually calm.

'Have you put any money on Lance?' she whispered. In spite of his connection with the racing industry, Declan didn't seem to be much of a punter.

'Oh, just a few hundred dollars each way. I'm not so much of a betting man,' he said, almost voicing her thoughts although he paused a moment before going on. 'Unlike my Uncle Tavis, who has placed a large bet with an Australian bookmaker online.'

'How large?'

'You don't think he'd tell me, do you?' Declan pulled a wry face. 'But we'll never hear the last of it now if Lance doesn't win.'

'But he can't — he knows it's a long shot and surely he doesn't expect . . . ?' Laura allowed her question to hang in the air.

'My uncle's expectations have never been realistic. He seems to think that the world — and God — owe him a living. I can only do my best to give him what he wants and sometimes that isn't easy.'

Laura stared at him, only now realizing how heavy was the weight of expectation Declan had to carry.

'You'll be all right here for a moment while I go down to the horse?' he murmured. 'I need to give Simon last-minute instructions and I want Jodie to come up here to watch the race.'

'Sure.' She smiled up at him. How thoughtful he was to think of the feelings of Lance's strapper when he had so much else to worry about today.

Outside, the twenty-four jockeys were lining up on stage to be introduced to the crowd, some of the younger ones shivering with nerves as well as the cold as their silks fluttered in the high wind. Introduced first and wearing Tavis Martin's distinctive colours of burgundy and white stripes, Simon Grant stood out very clearly from the crowd. Mercifully, there was a gap between the showers.

As the horses entered the mounting yard for their final parade, excitement mounted in the crowd. Twenty-four beautiful animals in the peak of condition and each at the pinnacle of his or her career. So much hope and so many dollars invested although everyone knew there could be only one winner.

Lancelot's Pride, used to both crowds and to racing in wet conditions, walked with his head held high, showing only mild interest in the noisy people taking photographs and calling out all around him. Declan arrived in time to give last-minute instructions to Simon and give him a leg up into the saddle. As he eased himself into the stirrups, encouraging and reassuring Lance that he was in safe hands, the jockey looked down at his fiancée, smiling into her eyes. Returning his smile, she looked up with all the love that she felt for him shining back.

'May the luck of the Irish go with you, Simon,' she whispered. 'I love you so much.'

'Love you, too,' He whispered back, blushing furiously. Only she knew what it had cost him to say so; Simon was a man of few words. Saluting Declan, he turned the big horse to lead the field out on to the track for the running of the Melbourne Cup.

'Nothing more for us to do, Jodie,' Declan sighed. 'It's all up to Simon now. Come on. You might as well join us up in the stands.'

'Like this?' She pulled a face, looking down at her dripping raincoat.

'Who cares? I'm sure I don't and neither will Laura. You've worked as hard as anyone to prepare Lance for the Cup and deserve to see him win.'

'Do you really think he can? John Partridge and the English stables think they're in with a chance.'

'They always boast that no one can touch them. Just because their owners have more money than anyone else. Money doesn't count for everything. More often than not, they're proved wrong.' He saw for the first time that Jodie was shivering. 'But you're freezing. You need to come in and have a drink to warm up.'

Following him into the stands, Jodie couldn't tell him that it was nerves rather than the chill that was making her shiver. She had heard one of the jockeys talking as he came off the previous race. 'Dangerous!' he had pronounced. 'If it rains any more, it'll be like a skating rink out there. I'm just as happy I don't have a ride in the Cup.' She knew this was partly sour grapes but there was an element of truth in his words. She wanted Simon to win for Declan — of course she did — but above all, she wanted him safe.

9

There was no time for further speculation as the field was on its way. Although Declan remained outwardly calm, Laura was aware of his intense concentration on the race as, rather than watch the progress of the horses on the television screen, he followed the race through a pair of binoculars, speaking to no one. Mentally, he was out there with Simon every step of the way. Too nervous and keyed up to take a seat either, Jodie went down and joined others watching the race from the window at the front of the stands. She glanced at the darkening sky, seeing the rain had just started again and, without realizing what she was doing, chewed her fingernails. Ironically, while most of Australia was still suffering from drought conditions, the skies had decided to open in Melbourne today.

To begin with, the pace was slow. Nobody wanted to be blinded by mud from the hooves of those racing ahead but neither did anyone care to throw down a challenge by taking the lead. The race caller seemed almost disappointed that he was unable to build more excitement into his commentary at this stage.

'No change in the order,' he droned, pointing out the positions of favoured horses. 'Christmas Fairy leads, followed by the English mare, Westminster Belle, Hope's Angel and College Kid close behind. Midfield, on the fence, is the Irish stayer, Lancelot's Pride.'

'What's he doing?' Declan muttered through clenched teeth. 'Not following my instructions. I told Simon to hang back and stay out of trouble and there he is, letting himself get trapped on the fence midfield.'

Laura tried to reassure him with a gentle pressure on his sleeve, feeling the tension in the muscles beneath her hand. 'Don't worry,' she said. 'Simon knows both the course and the conditions. You can trust him to make the right decisions.'

'Let's hope so.' Declan shrugged. 'It's in his hands and there's nothing I can do about it now.'

The field passed the winning post for the first time and there was little change in the order except that Christmas Fairy was already tiring and dropping back, letting Westminster Belle take up the lead. Immediately, she put several lengths between herself and the field travelling behind her.

'No-o!' Nearby, Declan heard John Partridge groan as if he were in pain. 'The idiot! She'll run out of puff! He's going too soon.'

Excitement mounted and the roar of the crowd increased as the wall of animals strained to improve position on reaching the final turn before the straight. After such a long race, only the fittest could hope to lift their game enough to gain a place. Most of them left the inside rail for what they hoped would be firmer ground in the middle of the track. At this point there was no clear leader; it was still anybody's race.

Only Simon remained on the inside as he began to urge Lance forward, asking for more speed. The big horse responded at once and Simon could tell he was in with a chance as he passed many horses who had already given their all, too tired to respond to his challenge. Now, he could see only one horse in front of him — Westminster Belle.

He had just reached her and was about to pass on the inside when she missed her footing and stumbled into him, breaking Lancelot's stride. There was a concerted groan from the crowd. Watching in horror, Jodie bit her knuckles, stifling a shriek. In conditions such as these, if anyone should fall, they were likely to be trampled by the wall of horses behind. Fortunately, both jockeys were experienced and good enough horsemen to ensure that they stayed in the saddle. Once the field had thundered past, Westminster Belle's rider stopped and dismounted, quick to realize that she was lame, while Simon encouraged Lance to get into his stride again.

But precious seconds had been lost. Two local horses overtook him swiftly to claim first and second place in a photo finish, the winning jockey screaming with excitement and waving his whip as he passed the winning post. Simon had to be content with bringing Lance into third place. Jodie, Declan and Laura all rushed down to meet him.

On the way, they passed John Partridge, surrounded by his group of disgruntled owners, demanding an explanation for Westminster Belle's lack of stamina and form. He looked like a man expecting to be lynched. Their other horse had finished nowhere, almost last.

'Well done, you beautiful boy!' As Simon dismounted, Jodie took charge of Lancelot's Pride, delighted to see them both uninjured and safe. 'Third place in a Melbourne Cup is nothing to be ashamed of.'

'We could have won.' Simon looked pained. 'I was so close, I could almost taste it. Sorry, Declan. If it hadn't been for that horse breaking down — '

'No regrets.' Declan was quick to reassure him. 'These things happen in racing, Simon. I'm not unhappy with this result. You did the best you could on a difficult day.'

Still rueful and shaking his head, Simon went to weigh in and face the television reporters who were always eager to hear the jockeys' comments after a major race. Jodie, still patting Lance and praising him for his efforts, led the horse back to his quarters to clean off most of the mud and give him a drink.

With Jodie and Simon out of earshot, Declan let his expression slip, allowing only Laura to see his disappointment. He glanced at his watch.

'No point in putting off the evil hour.' He grimaced. 'My uncle will have watched the race on TV and already know the result but he'll be looking for an explanation from me.'

'He can't be displeased?' Laura stared at him. 'Daniel was saying how hard it is even to get a horse accepted to run in the Cup. It's a wonderful achievement to get third place and the prize money will surely cover all his expenses?'

'You and I might see it that way, Laura, but my uncle will not. He put far too much money on Lance, expecting a win, and he will have lost it. I told him the competition was stiff and warned him to play it safe by backing the horse each way but he wouldn't listen. He said if I didn't expect to win, then I didn't deserve to be his representative overseas and he'd be looking to replace me with someone who had a more positive mental attitude.'

'That's so unfair. If Westminster Belle hadn't broken down and crashed into him, I'm sure Lance would have won.'

'But he didn't, did he? And my uncle's pockets will be considerably lighter.' He glanced at his watch. 'If it's OK with you, I'd rather leave. I haven't the heart to watch any more racing and Jodie will see to Lance and settle him in his quarters for the night. We'll go back to the motel and I can ring Tavis from there — he detests mobiles.'

'I won't let you mope. We *are* going to celebrate, aren't we?'

'Of course. Daniel's already booked a table at that Chinese restaurant. Jodie and Simon will be there, too — officially celebrating their engagement. But I won't be able to enjoy myself until I've spoken to the old man. Have to get that out of the way first.'

On arrival at Declan's motel, they ran into John Partridge, who greeted them with a sheepish smile, tie half undone and looking a little the worse for wear.

'What can I say?' He shrugged. 'You had the race in the bag. If it hadn't been for my horse breaking down — '

'And if she hadn't broken down, she might well have held on and won. No use crying about what might have been, John. The race is over and neither of our horses got the prize.'

'I was so sure of her, too.' John was talking half to himself. 'Of course, the owners want a scapegoat and they're blaming me for their loss. Said I hadn't spent enough time getting her strong enough for such a gruelling race.'

Declan wouldn't be unkind enough to say so but he thought this was probably a valid criticism. John had spent far more late nights enjoying the amenities of Melbourne than getting up early to supervise the track work of the horses in his charge. Even now, he was preparing to go out on the town.

Inside, Declan switched on the TV, turned up the volume, and left Laura sitting on the couch to watch it while he went into the bedroom to make the call to his uncle. His Aunt Maureen answered the phone.

'I don't know that you should speak to him right now,' she whispered, sounding almost fearful. 'I think you did very well to get third place but your uncle's been up all night drinking and he's fit to be tied.'

'I'll talk to him anyway, Auntie Mo.' He called her by the old, familiar nickname he had used as a child. 'If he gives me the sack, at least I'll know where I stand.'

'Oh, Declan, surely it won't come to that?'

'Don't be too sure. I've never known why but Tavis has never really liked me. This will give him the perfect excuse to be rid of me for good.'

'Maureen! Who is it?' Declan heard his uncle bellowing from somewhere in the background. 'Give me the phone. If it's that no-good whelp from Australia, I want to give him a piece of my mind.'

He heard his aunt trying to pacify the old man. 'Now Tavis, calm down. You're red as a turkey and you know what the doctor said about flying into these rages. It's bad for your blood pressure — '

'Damned old fool with his half-arsed quackery. What does he know?'

'Obviously a helluva lot more than you!'

Declan's eyes widened. He knew how unusual it was for his aunt to stand up to his uncle or swear even mildly.

'Go on then,' she said, handing over the phone. 'Work yourself into a state and take it out on poor Declan but I'm not staying around to hear it.'

Silence followed, apart from his uncle fumbling with the phone and finally getting it to his ear, confirming his aunt's observation that the old man was well on the way to being drunk.

'Well?' Tavis snapped. 'What have you got to say for yourself?'

'Only that I'm proud of both Lance and our team. We got third place.'

'Tell me something I don't already know. Third place, indeed. No one remembers third place getters. I sent you down there to win.'

'I know that, Nunc.' Deliberately, Declan used the nickname he knew Tavis hated. It angered him that the team's care and hard work should be so summarily dismissed. 'Lance was in peak condition and well prepared for the race. But you can't allow for interference or a horse breaking down.'

'I knew I should have sent the experienced rider. At least he'd have known enough to stay out of harm's way.'

'Well, it's easy to be wise after the race is over and I'm sorry you can't congratulate us. Everyone worked very hard here and it was a good enough result on a difficult day.'

'Who is it good enough for? Not me, nephew, I can assure you.'

Hearing his uncle refer to him in this way, Declan sighed. As far as Tavis Martin was concerned, he would never be more than a nephew, an unwanted presence in his house. Only his Aunt Maureen loved him as if he were her own son. He knew *that* didn't endear him to Tavis, either.

'OK, then,' he said, becoming businesslike. 'There's not a whole lot more we can do here. We might as well bring Lance home.'

'I don't want him back here. Why should I waste money transporting him home? A horse that can't even win a race against a bunch of their local nags.'

'And strong overseas competitors, including the Japanese.'

'Hah!' This was an expression of his uncle's scorn.

'You should know that Australian and New Zealand bred horses are among the finest in the world. If you could see — '

'Never mind your excuses. I don't care. Offer the horse for sale and take whatever you can get for him there.'

Hearing this, Declan felt as if his heart had sunk to his boots. He loved Lancelot's Pride; he was a brave and beautiful horse with a will to win that was rare. He didn't deserve to be sold off as if he had failed.

'Uncle Tavis, please don't make this decision while you're — um — well, not on the spur of the moment. When you get over your disappointment, I'm sure you'll see that — '

'All I see is that I have been let down!' the old man roared, making Declan wince and hold the phone away from his ear. 'Sell the horse and get your sorry arse back here. I'll decide what to do with you then.'

'What about Jodie?'

'What about her? She's a good enough strapper. There'll always be a job for her here.'

Declan flinched as the phone was hung up in his ear. 'Always a job for Jodie but not necessarily for me,' he muttered, trying to weigh up his situation if the worst happened and it came to finding another job. On the plus side, he had the trainer's licence his uncle had helped him acquire when he left for Australia but at the same time he couldn't trust his uncle to give him a fair recommendation in order to use it. He'd be lucky if he could get work as a stable hand. He waited a moment or two to compose himself before returning to Laura, who was pretending to be absorbed in a travel show on TV with the volume turned down.

She looked up, quick to interpret his 'too bright' smile.

'It didn't go well, then?'

''Fraid not. But he's not going to spoil our

evening.' He clapped his hands with false heartiness. 'We're going out on the town. You deserve to be seen in that fabulous dress.'

'No, Declan, don't shut me out. Tell me what happened. What did your uncle say?'

'Far too much. It's even worse than I expected. He's refusing to pay for Lance to go home and wants me to sell him to somebody here. I don't know how to tell Jodie — she'll be devastated.'

'That's miserable. Just when she has so much to celebrate, too.'

Declan's shoulders tensed. 'I need a drink — a real one.' He went to a cupboard and took out an unopened bottle of Bushmills and two glasses. 'You?'

She shook her head. 'I get silly after half a glass of champagne. But don't let me stop you.'

'You won't,' he said, pouring a generous measure into a glass and tossing it off without water or ice; the response of most men to bad news. From the grimace that followed, Laura decided he wasn't too used to drinking straight alcohol either. 'Ha, that's better.' His shoulders dropped and he relaxed, letting go a deep breath and pulling Laura into his arms although he didn't attempt to kiss her. 'Mm, you feel good. Smell good, too.'

She looked at him from under her brows,

ready for flight. 'Don't tell me you can still smell Eileen's perfume?'

'No. Just healthy young woman and good soap.'

She too relaxed and they remained there for several minutes, taking comfort from their embrace.

'Declan,' she said, after being lost in thought for a while. 'I don't really know much about horses or what goes into their training and I know you don't want to think about losing Lance — not tonight. But as we're seeing Daniel and Foxie, perhaps you should mention it. They're always on the lookout for good horses and maybe they could buy Lance? You know he'd be treated like a prince and he'd love it down there on the coast. And — and he'd still be in the family, sort of, wouldn't he? My family, anyway.'

'Laura, it's a lovely idea. But I don't want to put Daniel on the spot. He doesn't usually train up stayers — '

Laura leaned back out of his arms to look up at him. 'I know but he might like to start? Lance could be his first.'

'It's a lot more complicated than that.' Declan smiled and pulled her close again, kissing the top of her head. 'Trainers specialize. But if I can bring the subject up naturally, I'll mention it. They might recommend a buyer. I'd rather that than let him go to someone completely unknown.' He glanced at his watch. 'Hey, look at the time. Better go and freshen up, if you want to. We're due at the restaurant in just over half an hour.'

In the bathroom, Laura frowned at her tangled mane of hair. The rain and wind at the track had ruined any semblance of style. She wished she could have gone home, washed it again and dried it with the brush roller she used to straighten and tame her wayward locks. Instead, she had to make do by dragging a comb through the tangle of curls. As a rule, she didn't wear much make-up but she renewed it anyway, quickly, finishing with a pink lip gloss and a touch of eye liner to enhance the exceptionally dark blue of her eyes. Declan's expression when she returned was all she needed to know that she looked well.

Daniel's favourite Chinese restaurant was packed and busy. Many people in the racing industry had cause for celebration tonight. If Daniel had not booked a large table months in advance, there would have been no chance of accommodating such a big party.

A cheer went up as Laura and Declan were shown to Daniel's table, the last to arrive.

Seating twelve, it took up the entire corner of the room. Declan smiled and made a thumbs up sign to Jodie and Simon, who were already there. Jodie grinned in return, eyes sparkling with happiness and champagne. Not wanting to ruin her evening, he decided to wait as long as he could before telling her of his uncle's decision. However gently he broke the news, he knew she would be upset.

The waiter made sure the newcomers were seated comfortably and supplied them with flutes of champagne. With his table complete, Daniel rose to his feet to address his guests. 'Good to see you,' he said. 'Now the evening can really begin. Tonight, we have much to celebrate. In the early part of the day we had a nice win for our stables with Foxie's Fancy.' He smiled across the table, raising his glass to Foxie who inclined her head and smiled back, blowing him a kiss. Tonight she looked well rested and radiant, proudly displaying her growing pregnancy in a midnight-blue silk jersey gown which fell from her shoulders, flattering her figure. Even in pregnancy, she had a genius for making the best of herself.

'We have high hopes for our Fancy,' Daniel said. 'She's a big girl with everything in all the right places — the neck of a duchess and the solid arse of a cook.'

Laughter followed this remark although

some of them knew it wasn't original. 'And don't let's forget Declan, Simon and Jodie. who all worked so hard with Lancelot's Pride to achieve third place in the Melbourne Cup. A magnificent effort. Congratulations to all of you.' They all sat there beaming as the toast was drunk, followed by murmurs of agreement and applause. 'And to Laura, who is just nineteen today — many happy returns.'

Laura blushed and smiled; she hadn't expected anyone to remember that it was her birthday today.

'Why didn't you say?' Declan said in an agonized whisper. 'I didn't get you anything — not even a bunch of flowers.'

'It's OK — really.' She squeezed his hand. 'There has been so much else going on today.'

Still on his feet, Daniel was moving on to his final toast. 'And last but by no means least, we have Jodie and Simon — celebrating their engagement tonight.' He raised his glass again to encourage the assembled company to do the same. 'To the happy couple — congratulations and all our good wishes for a long and contented life.'

Even when he was done, other people stood up and many more toasts were made and drunk and by the time the food arrived, everyone was ready to do justice to the fabulous Asian feast.

The meal commenced with platters of cold meat, followed by shark's fin soup. Following the soup came various meat dishes in rich sauces — lobster, pork in fine delicious slices outlined in crimson, scallops and chicken and of course Peking duck, which no banquet would be complete without. There was choice enough for anyone's taste to be satisfied and the final savoury course was an enormous poached whole fish. Sweets followed although by now everyone was patting over-full stomachs, declaring that they couldn't possibly eat anything more.

When the formal dining was finally over, everyone moved, changing places to talk to those who had not been their dinner companions. Daniel took the opportunity to speak to Declan while Laura went to exchange a few words with Foxie.

'I've been watching you,' Daniel said. 'You're very quiet tonight. Are you all right?'

Declan smiled ruefully. 'I'm sorry. I was hoping it didn't show.'

'Laura hasn't come to her senses, then? Still turning you down?'

'No, it's not Laura, she's been great — a good friend. Very supportive.'

'Then what's wrong? After today's success, you should be over the moon.'

Declan sighed. 'I was. But, rather as I expected, my uncle is not.'

'Why, the miserable old devil.' Daniel's temper rose with indignation. He hated ingratitude and injustice of any kind. 'What did he expect?'

'I didn't want to talk about it tonight — spoiling the party.'

'Don't worry, no one's listening.' Daniel glanced around. Expansive, after a good meal, the other guests seemed involved in animated discussions of their own. 'Whatever you tell me will stay just between ourselves.'

'I called my uncle this afternoon. That was my first mistake — he'd been drinking all night before and after the race. They show it live on TV in the early hours of the morning. Eejit that I am, I should've waited until later tonight when he would have been sober and rested. Given him enough time to get over it.'

'Get over what? Third place is no mean achievement against a Melbourne Cup field. Praise and congratulations were in order, I'd say.'

'Not from my uncle. He's angry and disappointed as well as out of pocket. I told him the competition was stiff but he still put all his money on Lance's nose. He doesn't punt very often but when he does, he plunges big time.'

'More fool him, then.' Daniel had little sympathy for the stubborn old man.

'And now he's saying he doesn't want Lance to come home. I'm to sell him off and return to Ireland without him. Sooner rather than later.'

'That's just beer talk. He'll get over it, surely. And when he does — '

'You don't know my Uncle Tavis. His favourite pastime is cutting off his nose to spite his face.'

Daniel thought for a moment. 'Right now, as we stand at the moment, we'd have enough room to stable Lance down there on the coast — '

'Are you offering to buy him?' Declan's eyes widened in relief. 'That would be — '

'No, no. And certainly not without talking it over with Foxie.' Daniel was quick to explain. 'Don't get ahead of yourself. All I can offer you is a bit of breathing space. I know you don't think so now but your uncle might come to his senses and change his mind.'

'No.' Declan shook his head. 'Once he's made a decision, he'll never alter it.'

'You two look very solemn.' Foxie arrived, placing a hand on her husband's shoulder. 'You know what I said. You're not allowed to talk business tonight. Plenty of time for that in the morning.'

Briefly, Daniel explained the young Irishman's problem and the temporary solution of the big horse coming to stay with them on the coast.

'I have no problem with that,' Foxie said. 'He's a gelding, isn't he? We have mostly fillies and mares. A stallion in the mix might make everyone restless.' She wrinkled her nose.

'He's gelded all right — my uncle never keeps horses entire.' Declan assured her. 'He likes them to be more interested in racing than breeding. And Lance is a perfect gentleman — has no vices.'

'Then, yes. Bring him over whenever you like. Of course, it'll be more difficult for him to race in the city from down there.'

'That's OK. I can't afford the entry fees, anyway. Thank you so much, both of you.' Declan clasped their hands. 'You don't know what this means to me.'

'Only too happy to help.' Daniel smiled.

★ ★ ★

Laura meanwhile had joined a small clique of Irish people who had all been drinking enough to venture into song. A piano had been unearthed and, although it was well out of tune, one of the Irishmen was strumming the keys, belting out all the old favourites including 'Bye Bye Blackbird', 'When Irish Eyes Are Smiling' and finally 'I'll Take You Home Again, Kathleen'.

Declan, finding himself far from home and quite unable to resist such overt Irish sentimentality, forgot his troubles long enough to join in with a pleasing and surprisingly strong baritone.

As many of Daniel's guests were horsemen and women who would be able to snatch only a few hours' sleep before going to work, the party broke up long before midnight. Declan stood up, surprised to find he was a little unsteady on his feet.

'Sorry, Laura,' he said. 'I can't drive you — I've had far too much to drink.'

'Too much champagne.' She nodded, with a silly grin on her face. It was only then that he realized she had gone way beyond her customary half glass. She was in the euphoric phase. Hopefully, sleep rather than sickness would follow. 'I'll take a taxi and drop you off on my way home.'

'OK,' she said, too far gone to make any objections.

Although the journey in the taxi could not have taken more than ten minutes, by the time they arrived at Laura's apartment, she was sound asleep against Declan's shoulder, snoring gently. He groaned, knowing he'd have to see her indoors and, if no one else was home, even put her to bed.

'Bad luck, mate.' The taxi driver grinned as he pocketed his fare. 'Looks like that one's out for the count tonight.'

Carrying the dead weight of Laura up the steps to her apartment, Declan staggered, a little the worse for drink himself. What had possessed him? He didn't even like champagne.

Although it was late to be making a noise, he leaned on the doorbell for at least twenty seconds, hearing it peal loudly somewhere inside. Surely one of the girls would be there, even if Eileen was working late at the pub. He rang impatiently, several more times, but nobody came.

'Laura!' He started to shake her, none too gently. 'Do you have your key in your purse?'

'Key,' she muttered, simpering in her sleep. 'Key. Kiki. Silly word.'

'Laura, we're both going to look silly if you don't find it. Stuck out here on the steps until Eileen comes home.'

'Oh Declan!' She wove her arms around his neck and gave him a smacking kiss on the cheek. 'It must be at Foxie's. In my other bag.' She sounded quite unconcerned.

'Well, great,' he muttered under his breath.

'I'll have to take you to my place.'

'Your place,' she murmured. 'Yes, please.' And she dropped her head on his shoulder, asleep again almost immediately.

Fortunately, the taxi who had just dropped them off had not yet been hired. Declan hailed it again and with a look that invited no comment, he briefed the driver on the location of his motel. Fortunately, the man knew it and needed no further directions. On arrival at their destination, he grinned, ready to make another smart remark, until Declan silenced him with a steely look, daring him to say anything.

10

He unlocked his front door before returning for Laura, grateful that neither John Partridge nor any of the other horsemen were around to see him lifting her from the back of the cab. He could do without ribald comment from anyone.

Inside, he laid her on his bed, took off her shoes and helped her out of her jacket that had somehow become tangled around her, all askew. She frowned and muttered in her sleep but she didn't wake up. He considered helping her out of her dress but decided not to disturb her further. If she happened to wake while he was undressing her, she would be sure to think the worst, especially after the episode in that garden in the hills; he could cringe at the memory even now. So he tucked her in and covered her up, fully dressed.

After that, he prepared to do the gentlemanly thing and sleep on the sitting-room couch although it was far too short to give him a decent night's rest. He grabbed a pillow and some extra blankets for a makeshift bed before stripping down to his singlet and shorts; he had no intention of crushing his only good suit.

Uncomfortable as it was, with the pillow in his arms, he was just about to drift off into an uneasy sleep when an anguished cry from Laura brought him fully awake.

'Declan, help! I think I'm going to be sick!'

This galvanized him into action. Seconds later he was hauling her towards the bathroom, hoping they'd make it in time. As luck would have it, they did. He supported Laura's forehead while she leaned on his hand and vomited into the toilet like a child, without inhibition and losing everything she had eaten and drunk that night. Fortunately, he was used to this routine, having done the same thing for many a lad in his uncle's stables who had overestimated his capacity for ale on a Saturday night.

'Better now?' he said, handing Laura a box of tissues when the convulsions finally stopped.

She took a deep breath, wiped the tears from her eyes and blew her nose, still shivering from the experience. 'Not a very romantic end to the evening,' she said, managing a brief smile. 'Thanks for being so understanding.'

'That's OK.' He gave her back a final, comforting rub. 'But you'll think twice before drinking too much next time.'

'There won't be a next time. I'm sworn off the drink for ever.'

'Oh, yeah? That's what they all say.'

'My mouth tastes foul. I don't suppose you have a spare toothbrush?'

'Sure do.' He opened the bathroom cabinet and offered one, still in the plastic wrapper.

Laura took it and then frowned. 'What other preparations do you make for unexpected visitors?'

'This is it. I hate being caught without a new toothbrush.' He shrugged. 'Don't build too much into it.'

She cleaned her teeth vigorously, spat and then rinsed just as vigorously. 'That's better.' She ran her tongue over her teeth and looked at them in the mirror. Her normal colour was starting to return. 'I do so hate being sick.'

'Maybe we can get some sleep now?' Declan looked longingly at his makeshift bed. 'I have to be up early to talk to Jodie about Lance. I'm not looking forward to it.'

'I am sorry.' Laura chewed her lip. 'I'm a real nuisance, aren't I?'

'No.' He smiled at her. 'You're just Laura being her usual impulsive self.'

'Can you unzip me?' She turned her back towards him. 'I can't really sleep in this dress.'

Declan unfastened the zipper, seeing from the expanse of creamy flesh that appeared underneath it that she had been wearing no bra. 'I'll leave you to it, then.' He muttered, glancing towards the sitting room and the uncomfortable night he faced on the couch.

'Please don't leave me,' she said in a small voice. 'Sure'n there has to be plenty of room for both of us in that king-sized bed. You won't get any proper sleep on that couch.'

'That's all very well, but — '

'It's all right. I trust you.'

'Maybe so. But can I trust myself? Look at you — sitting half naked there. Enough to drive a man to distraction.'

'Then lend me a shirt to sleep in.'

He found one and offered it to her at arm's length, averting his gaze.

Laughing at such exaggerated propriety, she put the shirt on, rolled up the sleeves and then hopped into bed, sighing with contentment as she snuggled in. Although she was still hot and flushed, she was feeling much better after losing the cause of her malaise. But Declan was in no hurry to get in beside her and continued to stand there, looking unsure.

'Come on, get in.' She patted the pillow beside her. 'You said yourself you have to be up early.'

Still he hesitated. 'Laura, this isn't a good idea.'

'Oh, I see.' Her lips trembled and her eyes filled with incipient tears. 'You're put off now, aren't you? Now you've seen me being sick.'

'Lord, no. How could you think I'd be so shallow.'

That wasn't the matter, not at all. Earlier in the day, before speaking to his uncle, he had been thinking of asking Laura to marry him, even allowing himself to hope that she would accept. But how could he offer anyone marriage right now when he might be out of a job? It was all very well that in this brand new century there was a lot of talk about equality between the sexes but Laura was the old-fashioned sort; a woman made for marriage rather than a career. No. He couldn't expect her to marry him now when his future remained so uncertain. It wouldn't be fair.

'Suit yourself, then.' She turned away, misunderstanding his reluctance and composing herself for sleep.

Gingerly, he climbed into bed beside her, finding her sullen posture less daunting than her previous attitude. At once, she curled herself into a tighter ball, moving as far away from him as she could.

'Laura, please.' Cautiously, he reached out to rest a hand on her shoulder, finding that although she had expelled most of the toxins from her body, she was still very hot and feverish to the touch. 'Don't be upset. You're still not quite well — maybe running a temperature,' he whispered, dropping a kiss on her exposed shoulder — his shirt was much too large for her. 'We should get some sleep.'

But instead of agreeing with him and relaxing into position for sleep, she shocked him by turning into his embrace, winding her arms about his neck and moulding herself against the whole length of his body before kissing his throat and making him gasp. She had taken him by surprise, the unnatural heat of her body exciting him and setting them both on fire.

'Oh, Laura,' he groaned. 'Just don't — '

'Ssh!' she whispered, nipping the lobe of his ear and sending a jolt of pleasure through him and instigating desire as she pushed up his singlet to run her hands over his chest. Her touch was so sure that he had to force himself to remember that she was a virgin and he should take it slow. She seemed to know so exactly how to arouse him, even gently pinching his nipples to show him what she would like him to do to her own. She couldn't know what she was doing — or did she? Perhaps, after all, she was more experienced than she had led him to believe.

He had no further time for thought as desire took hold of him and his body responded. He felt flushed all over as if he were catching her feverish heat and he flung off the bedclothes to lean over her, tearing aside the shirt that separated his body from her own. He had to have her now; there would be no turning back.

Her eyes widened at the size of his erection and he knew she must be startled by his extreme reaction to her teasing but passion had him in its grasp and he was beyond gentleness now. He kissed her deeply and fiercely, still half waiting for her to push him away and ask him to stop. But although he could sense she was nervous, she wasn't unwilling and allowed him to part her legs, prior to making love. She gasped and held on tightly, whimpering only a little as he entered her; she seemed unusually small. She bit his ear even more sharply this time, teasing the shell with the tip of her tongue. *Who on earth had taught her to do that?* Groaning with pleasure, he thrust further, aware of her tightness and realizing at some level of his consciousness that in spite of her expertise in the art of heavy petting, she was indeed a virgin. And now, now that he had unlocked her passion, Laura was quick to find her own rhythm, quivering with excitement as she moved her body seductively against his own.

With a cry of triumph, he came inside her, realizing too late that there should have been some protection. He just hadn't thought of it until it was too late. Never a promiscuous man, Declan had been intimate only with Lucy, who had taken charge of matters of birth control. To be sure, Lucy wanted to start a family but certainly not out of wedlock. She had been careful to the point of ruining any spontaneity in their love-making. But Laura was someone else entirely; there was nothing of calculation in her nature and she gave herself to him joyously and without inhibition. A prize indeed, deserving better than to be married to an out-of-work stable hand. Tonight was a gift, a brief respite from the misery his life was likely to be, at least in the short term.

'Oh, Laura, you are so wonderful — beautiful,' he managed to whisper into her hair as post-coital drowsiness finally claimed him. Vaguely, he was aware of her leaving the bed to go to the bathroom. When she came back, he knew she would want to talk and he had every intention of staying awake to do so. But it had been such a long day that sleep finally claimed him before she did.

The next thing he knew was the insistent hum of the alarm on his watch at 4.30 a.m.

He turned it off quickly and glanced across at Laura, hoping it hadn't disturbed her. She murmured in her sleep but didn't wake up.

He lay there for a moment, staring at the ceiling, thinking of all that he had to do that day and trying not to feel so guilty about Laura. In the cool light of early morning, he knew he shouldn't have taken advantage of her vulnerability. The fact that he was seriously in love with her was still no excuse. So where did they go from here? Now they were lovers, she might take that as a commitment but really nothing had changed. He was still a man without prospects or any secure future.

And now there was Jodie to think about and Lancelot's Pride. He would have to hire a float to take the champion down to the Morgan stables on the coast. He knew that if he didn't move quickly, Tavis might grow impatient enough to offer the horse for sale while he was still stabled in town, leaving Declan no choice in the matter.

He showered quickly and quietly, dressed in his work clothes and stood looking down at Laura with his boots in his hand, ready to put on outside. She was sleeping soundly, lying on her back, breathing deeply, arms flung above her head, her abundant hair framing her face. To Declan she had never looked lovelier; he wanted to kiss her awake and make love to her all over again. But he resisted the temptation. Duty called.

He knew that she was supposed to start work herself at midday and would need to get back to town. A quick check of her purse showed she had less than ten dollars in small change — not nearly enough to get a taxi — public transport would take too long.

He scribbled a note on a scrap of paper, saying *Get a taxi home. Love you forever, D* and tucked it under her pillow together with three twenty-dollar notes. She murmured briefly, once more shifting in her sleep. Then, after leaving the lightest of kisses on her brow and making sure not to wake her, he crept from the room.

⋆ ⋆ ⋆

In the throes of a dream, Laura thrashed around, causing Declan's message and one of the twenty-dollar notes to slip down behind the mattress and land on the floor. She awoke briefly, saw that Declan was gone, and went back to sleep, her feverish state making her dream more vividly than ever. She was still sleeping when, around half past ten, a maid came in to do the rooms, scarcely able to hide her amusement at finding a woman in

Declan's bed. A weary-looking blonde in her early twenties, she waved for Laura to stay where she was.

'Go back to sleep if you want. I can come back later,' she said.

'Ooh no. Look at the time.' Laura sprang out of bed and immediately wished she hadn't as her brains seemed to be loose in her head and the sun streaming in as the maid threw back the curtains was painful to her eyes. Her body was still punishing her for drinking too much champagne. 'I have to be at work by twelve. The boss goes bananas if we're late.'

'Don't they all?' The girl nodded sympathetically. 'You get a shower, then, and I'll start in here.'

When Laura returned from the shower, feeling a little better, the girl was putting the finishing touches to the newly made bed. Laura tried not to look at the bundle of stained and rumpled sheets on the trolley, reminding her of virginity well and truly lost.

'Oh and by the way,' the girl said, handing her two twenty-dollar notes. 'I found these under your pillow. Did you leave them there?'

'No.' Laura stared at the notes before taking them. 'It must have been — But wasn't there any message with them? Any note?'

'Sorry.' The girl pulled a wry face. 'Men

221

— all the same. Think they can buy you off with a few dollars. The very devil, aren't they?'

Laura didn't answer but sank down on the bed, at a loss for words. Was it really like that? On second thoughts, she didn't think so. Declan would have known she needed to get to the Leprechaun by noon and had been thoughtful enough to leave her this money to do so. But where were the words of endearment she craved — the promise of when he would see her again? He had left her money when she needed reassurance and proof of his love. Only now, in her mind, did she hear her mother's warning. *Give yourself too easily and a man won't respect you.* In Ireland, every time Laura went out with a different boy, Bridie had repeated this phrase like a mantra. Laura had been impatient with her mother, thinking her old-fashioned to the point of being quaint, but now she wondered if there might have been something in it. *A man will drop you soon as he's had what he wants.* That was another favourite saying and Laura wished she didn't have to remember it now.

As she sat there, reliving the events of the previous night, she remembered that she had been the one who insisted on sharing the bed; Declan had been quite willing to sleep on the couch. Of course, it was inevitable that they should make love. She cast her mind back, trying to remember exactly how it had happened but she had been feverish and her memory was hazy. The love-making hadn't been easy at first, she remembered that much, but once that initial barrier had been surmounted, it had been all right. Or so she had thought. But maybe she was mistaken. Declan wasn't a cruel man and he had hidden his feelings well but clearly she must have disappointed him with her naïvety and incompetence as a lover. No wonder he didn't bother to leave a note.

She was shaken from these thoughts by the clock in the room informing her that it was nearly half past eleven. She tucked the money into her purse and slung Foxie's jacket over her shoulder. Then she telephoned for a taxi and went outside to wait for it. She needed fresh air.

Behind her, inside the motel, the maid finished tidying the sitting room and was now collecting waste paper to put in the bin. She bent down to pick up a newspaper sticking out from under the bed and peered underneath to see if there was anything more. There she found Declan's message still wrapped around the remaining twenty-dollar note. She snatched them up and ran to the door, meaning to hand them to Laura but she was too late. She arrived just in time to see the taxi leaving the driveway to join the stream of traffic on the main road.

She thought of leaving the note and the money somewhere in plain sight but decided against it. If no one came back to claim it, the maid who turned down the beds might not be as honest as she was. And as for Laura herself, wasn't she lucky enough? She already had Declan Martin; the man all the girls fancied and who was all the more gorgeous because he didn't seem to know it. So she screwed up the note, threw it away with the rubbish and pocketed the twenty-dollar note. Well, why not, she thought, tossing her lank, blonde hair. It had been a long time since anyone had given her a decent tip.

★ ★ ★

As Declan had predicted, Jodie was taking the news about Lance very badly. He caught up with her in the stables where she had already walked the big horse and was now feeding him. Lance munched on, oblivious to her distress.

'But Mr Martin can't do this to us — he just can't!' Stricken, she was wringing her hands. Her lips trembled as huge tears formed and splashed from her eyes unheeded. 'How can he think of selling Lance when — when he did so well? It's not fair!' Her words came out between hiccoughing sobs. 'I can't — be parted from him. I — love him so much.'

'Goes without saying. So do I.' Declan put his arm around the little strapper and gave her a squeeze. She felt small and vulnerable, quite unlike her usual bouncy self. He understood how she felt; she had been Lance's strapper ever since she came to Tavis Martin's stables as a girl just out of school. He wished that Simon could have been there; he might've known how to comfort her. But Simon was busy with track work elsewhere. She pulled away from him, hugging herself in her misery.

'This is not going to happen.' She sniffed and wiped her nose on the back of her hand. 'What can we do?'

'All might not be lost,' Declan tried to reassure her. 'Daniel Morgan is offering to keep him for me while we find the right buyer — '

'That won't take very long. Any fool can see he's a beautiful horse. Anyone except your stupid uncle.'

Declan didn't bother to contradict her. 'And after that Uncle Tavis is expecting us both back in Ireland — '

'No way. Not without Lance. What does he expect me to do?'

'Take care of some of his other horses, I suppose. He says there'll always be a job for you in his stables.'

'Oh, really? Well, he can stuff his job. If Lance is staying here in Australia — so am I.'

'Jodie, it might not be that simple,' he said, thinking of Laura. 'Lance will probably go to a high-profile stables — someone who already has enough strappers. And, even if you're getting married to Simon, you'll still need work permits and so on in order to stay here. And what about Simon himself? Isn't he already lining up work in Ireland?'

'Well, he can change his mind, can't he?' Jodie's mouth pursed in a sullen line. 'We can get married and stay here.'

He could see there was no point in arguing with Jodie in this mood. She had suffered a shock and would need some time to get over it.

As if on cue, the horse transport arrived, ready to spirit Lance away to the country. Insisting on travelling with him, Jodie found his rug and leg wraps before gathering together his food and the rest of his tack. While she was doing so, Declan made a quick call to the Morgan stables to make sure they would be able to accommodate Lancelot's strapper as well as the horse. Foxie, sounding cheerful, answered his queries.

'Don't worry, Declan,' she said. 'She can stay here with me at the house. It will be nice to have female company and I can do with an extra hand.'

As a dedicated horsewoman, Declan wasn't sure how much use Jodie was going to be in anyone's house but he didn't think this was the time to say so. Jodie's domestic shortcomings would come to light soon enough.

Fifteen minutes later, he was seeing them on their way. Waving cheerfully, Jodie was once more full of optimism, confident that a good solution to all their problems was about to be found. Declan waved back, wishing he could share her views.

* * *

Laura arrived at the Leprechaun just before twelve, surprised to see Eileen behind the bar. After working so late the previous night, her friend should have been having some well-earned time off. Instead she was behind the bar, looking pale and out of sorts.

'Thank goodness you're here.' She pulled a comic distressed face. 'Patrick's in a foul mood.'

'What's his problem?' Laura was in no

mood to be bullied by Patrick. 'And you shouldn't be here at all — it's your day off. Where's Emily?'

'Don't ask. I'll tell you all about it later.'

'Well, well, Laura!' Patrick said, catching sight of her as he came up from the cellar. 'Glad you could join us. You do know I expect our girls to be here fifteen minutes before the hour, so you're ready to start your shift on time?'

'Well, I'm here now, aren't I?' she snapped, unwilling to put up with Patrick's bad temper, especially today. Time had moved on and he had quickly forgotten the debt that he owed her. 'What will it be, gentlemen?' She pushed past him to serve a small crowd of Irish horsemen at the bar, recognizing some of them from the previous night. 'A healing pint of Guinness all round?'

But Patrick wasn't done. 'And I want a word with you later,' he said, tapping her on the shoulder and making her shrug away from him. 'To talk about work permits. There's something very funny been going on here.'

★ ★ ★

It was past three o'clock before Laura and Eileen had time to talk. They were clearing up after the lunchtime rush and Patrick had gone up to his apartment upstairs, for the moment forgetting his promise to speak to Laura.

'Why are you here today?' Laura could see that her friend was pale with exhaustion. 'You should be having a well-earned rest. Isn't this Emily's shift?'

'Emily's gone. Under a cloud. Immigration turned up last night at our busiest time and Patrick's in heaps of hot water — he could face charges for employing people who don't have proper work permits.'

'Uh-oh,' Laura said.

'They just laughed at Emily's — said it wasn't even a decent forgery. Emerald Green, indeed!'

'Emerald Green? Eileen, hello! That's the same one I used.'

'Yes and they're coming back. They told Patrick they want to see you, too.'

Laura's eyes widened.

'Don't panic just yet. I don't suppose they work on a Sunday.'

'No? They were working on Saturday night. So what happens to Emily now?'

'I dunno.' Eileen seemed remarkably unsympathetic. 'They'll probably hold her somewhere like prison or a detention centre until they deport her.'

'Prison? But that's awful — and it could

happen to me, too.'

'Why? You've still got your visitor's visa, haven't you? Long as they don't catch you actually working here. Patrick will fudge it for you and say you've already gone — he doesn't want any more trouble.'

'Eileen, wait a moment. You're going too fast.'

Eileen shrugged. 'Nobody needs to employ a detective to guess that you stayed with Declan last night. We all saw your bed wasn't slept in. It's simple. All you have to do is go back to Ireland, marry that lovely man and live happily ever after.'

'This isn't a fairytale, Eileen. I'm not even sure he wants to see me again, let alone marry me.'

'Oh, come on. You didn't make *that* much of a hash of it, did you?'

'Maybe I did. I don't know. I've nothing to measure it by.'

'You're suffering from virgin's remorse, that's all.' Eileen put her arm around Laura's shoulders and gave her a squeeze. 'Happens to all of us. No use cryin' over spilt milk — you can't put the clock back and be a virgin twice, you know.'

Laura laughed weakly. 'You're such a comfort, Eileen.'

'Now. You toddle off home and pack. You'll

find a tartan one under my bed if you need another bag.'

'Thanks.' Laura glanced anxiously at the stairs. 'But what about Patrick?'

'Never mind Patrick. I'll square it with him and collect your pay.'

'You're rushing me — I can't think.'

'You don't have to. Patrick's the one who's in trouble for hiring two girls with the name of Emerald Green. His only chance is to plead ignorance and stupidity. And if the second Emerald Green disappears without trace, who's going to connect her with one Laura Flanagan?'

Laura thought for a moment. 'Everyone knows I was sharing a flat with you girls. Where shall I go?'

Eileen rolled her eyes. 'Do I have to think of everything? Go to the flat, clear out your stuff and high-tail it to your cousin's place on the coast. If you go now, the flat should be empty and you won't even have to explain yourself. Then you can lie low there until Declan can come for you.'

'You seem very certain he will. And what about the small matter of my air fare? I've got some money but not enough to buy an airline ticket to Europe.'

'Either way, Laura, you're going back to Ireland whether you want to or not — you can do it the hard way or the easy way.'

'There's no easy way! Oh, if only I had more time. I haven't seen Declan since last night and I don't know how he — '

'Think about him later. You're running out of time. Just go before Patrick comes down again and the other girls get here. Biddie and Gill will be starting at four — '

'But what about you? You must be dead on your feet?'

'Not really. I'm so overtired, I couldn't sleep now if I wanted to.'

'Thank you, Eileen.' Laura's eyes filled with tears and her lips trembled. 'I don't know when I'll see you again. I shall miss you.'

'Yeah, but we haven't got time for sentiment.' Eileen fished in her purse and took out two crisp fifty-dollar notes. 'Public transport won't work on a Sunday — get yourself a taxi and pay me back when you can.'

Laura hugged her friend one more time, grabbed Foxie's jacket and the Chanel purse and ran for the door.

11

It didn't take Laura very long to pack; she had few possessions and not all that many clothes. She didn't even need to borrow the additional travel bag that Eileen had offered. She stared around her sparse, almost empty bedroom for the last time and sighed as she shut the door. She wasn't looking forward to the prospect of returning so precipitately to her homeland, having set off for Australia with such hopes, such plans. Inevitably, this led her to think of Bridie, who had been ominously silent for some time.

Before leaving, she decided to check her e-mails one last time, hoping there might be a message. Her heart lurched with pleasure when she saw that there was. Bridie had left this message two days ago but having been to the Cup and the celebrations afterwards, Laura had not been home to receive it.

My dearest Laura — I have some good news.

You'll be pleased to know I have escaped the clutches of Stanley Winton and I am on my way home! Yes, really! I'm sure you must be wondering how this miracle came about. From a very unexpected and unlikely source. Stanley's Aunt Cassie.

After I gave her scorched toast and burned grits for the second time this week — I never was much of a cook, as you know — she took me aside and said we needed to talk. 'Not happy with our Stanley, are you, girl?' she said to me. 'A contented woman doesn't massacre good food.' I wasn't sure where all this was leading until she offered to give me money to leave — 'Not for your sake, you understand,' she was quick to inform me. 'But so we can have a servant again with a proper understanding of Southern food.'

My expectations weren't high. I thought she'd give me a ten-dollar note and some change and expect me to make myself scarce on that. But she gave me this envelope that really did feel quite fat although I didn't dare look at it until I was sure Stanley wasn't about — or Fleur (dreadful woman — more about her another time). To my surprise, Aunt Cassie had given me in excess of five thousand dollars — how about that? She really did want to get rid of me, didn't she?

I could hardly wait until evening when Stanley and Fleur go out to their club.

Soon as they did, I called the local taxi and got as far away from that bayou as I could in a single night. I didn't waste time in Miami but took a cheap flight to New York where I went to this Internet café to write to you. And best news of all, Mr Sampson — Lord love the man! — is more than happy to give me my old job back. He says the sales of his agency have dropped like a stone without me. So-o, by the time you get this, I'll be on a flight to London and should be back in Ireland in less than a week.

Let me know what you are doing and if you're happy down there in Oz? If I do well with Sampson over the next six months, I might even manage a visit. As for men — trust me, darlin', this is the last time. You can give me a good slap if I look like getting married again.

Your ever-loving Mam.

Laura giggled, forgetting her own troubles for a while as she printed a copy of her mother's e-mail and read it again. This was much better. At least she wasn't going to be alone like an orphan in Ireland, nor would she have to throw herself on the mercy of old Auntie Kit.

She froze as her thoughts were interrupted

by an insistent pealing of the doorbell. What if those people from Immigration *did* work on a Sunday, after all? She tiptoed into the hall and looked through the spy hole to see who it was and could have wept with relief when she saw them. Just two little girls in brownie-scout uniform, looking expectantly at the door. Smiling, she opened it.

'We're selling sweets and raffle tickets to raise money for our pack,' said the elder girl. 'Which would you like?'

Laura inspected a tray of rather mauled-looking packets of sweets. 'Have you any chocolate?' she said, realizing that in her haste to leave the Leprechaun, she'd had nothing to eat.

Heads together, the children scratched about in the box to produce a couple of single bars. 'Don't you want any raffle tickets as well?' The elder brownie seemed a bit disappointed about the size of her sale.

'No, thank you,' Laura said firmly. 'I'm leaving just now and wouldn't be able to collect a prize, anyway.'

'You could still buy some,' the younger girl chipped in. 'You probably won't win, anyway.'

Laura laughed. 'Go on with you,' she said as she paid them, urging them on their way. 'I'm in a hurry now.'

Before summoning a taxi and leaving the flat for the last time, Laura called Daniel's house in town. It was just possible that he and Foxie might have stayed there after the party. Mrs Wicks answered the phone.

'Oh, Laura dear, you've just missed them. They were here but Mrs Morgan took off over an hour ago to drive down to the coast. Mr Morgan said he wanted to put in a few hours at the office but whether he's still there — '

Laura could have kissed the old lady for this good news. Hopefully, she could catch Daniel and discuss her predicament away from Foxie's disapproving gaze. Much as she adored her cousin's wife, she knew Foxie was uncompromising when it came to breaking or even bending the law. 'Thanks, Mrs Wicks,' she said, with a smile in her voice. 'Catch you later!'

Her spirits fell when a call to Daniel's office was picked up by a machine. She decided to keep talking anyway, in case he was still there.

'Daniel, it's Laura. Please pick up. Oh, please, please!'

'What is it, Laura?' Daniel's rather impatient voice came on the line. 'You sound a bit stressed.'

'Oh, Daniel, thanks be to Jesus you're there — '

'Jesus has nothing to do with it. I was just on my way out.'

'Please, Daniel — can I see you? I'm in such a terrible mess and I don't know what to do.' Laura took a deep breath as tears blocked her throat, making it hard to speak.

'Whoa, you really *are* in a state, aren't you?' Daniel said, a little more kindly. 'Where are you now? That untidy hovel you share with those other girls?'

'Yes,' Laura said, forced to smile through her tears.

'Wait there and I'll be with you in about fifteen minutes. You can make me some coffee and tell me all about it.'

Daniel arrived in about twenty minutes, complaining of difficulty in finding somewhere to park. Laura gave him the promised coffee and he listened, saying nothing until she had finished her whole sorry tale. On the brighter side, she mentioned that Bridie had escaped from the clutches of Stanley Winton and was already on her way back to Ireland. She thought better of telling Daniel that she had spent the night with Declan at his motel — better for him to think she had been here.

'Well, you don't do things by halves, Laura, do you?' he said when she came to the end of it, hoarse from talking for so long without a break. 'Out of a job and Immigration hot on your trail. I'm resisting the temptation to say I told you so.'

'Please do.' Laura winced. 'So what am I to do? Eileen says I should hide out with you and Foxie until some of the fuss dies down.'

'That's only putting off the evil hour. As I see it, Laura, you've blown it. You need to get on a plane back to Ireland before anyone makes the connection between Laura Flanagan and the second fictitious Emerald Green.'

'Oh but Eileen says they're not likely to — '

'Eileen's advice hasn't done you much good so far. Isn't she the one who got you into this pickle in the first place?'

'No, she's been wonderful. It was Eileen who found me the job and borrowed the work permit from Emily so I could — ' She stopped talking as Daniel silenced her with a raised eyebrow.

'And as I predicted, it has ended in tears. At least when you get back to Ireland, your mother will be there to look after you — you won't have to do everything on your own.'

'I don't need looking after,' Laura muttered, ignoring Daniel's raised eyebrow. She was wondering if it really would be possible for her to slip back into her old life with

Bridie. She was used to a measure of independence now and, in spite of her mother's fervent promises to the contrary, she was sure it wouldn't be long before another man came into Bridie's life.

'Good. Now let's get down to brass tacks — how much money do you have?'

'I have some savings. Not enough to get me a ticket to Ireland.'

'I'll buy it, then. You can't arrive destitute. Hopefully, I can get you on a plane within forty-eight hours.'

'So soon?'

'No point in delaying, is there? I'll call Foxie to let her know what's happening. She made me promise to be home for dinner — no chance of that now.'

'I'm sorry, Daniel. I've totally messed up your day.'

'It's a challenge, isn't it?' His smile was wolfish. 'We'll go back to Kew now and I'll call in a few favours to see how quickly I can get you on a plane.' He registered her less than happy expression. 'All right, what is it now? What haven't you told me?'

'Nothing,' she said in a small voice, daunted by her cousin's impatient, business-like attitude. 'It's just that I haven't seen Declan since last night and he won't know what I'm doing or where I am — '

'Then call him up on your mobile and tell him.'

'I can't. The battery's flat and I keep forgetting to charge it.'

Daniel sighed, exasperated, the more so because Foxie was always doing the same thing. Some women seemed to have no affinity with modern technology.

'Then use mine.'

Laura shook her head. 'There's too much to tell him and I don't know what to say.'

'OK. But we need to get going.' Having decided on a course of action, Daniel picked up Laura's bags and headed for the door. 'Leave your keys on the hall table,' he ordered. 'Whatever happens, you won't be coming back here.'

Laura followed him, still unaccountably miserable. It was good of Daniel to help her but she couldn't help feeling that he had taken over her life.

★ ★ ★

Having sent Jodie to accompany Lance to the Morgan stables on the coast, Declan was wondering if it had been wise to let her go alone. More than once, Daniel had confided that his wife was unusually touchy and sensitive right now and subject to moods. At the same time, Jodie had never been the most tactful of girls and it would make things awkward if the two women took a dislike to each other. But before taking off for the coast, he decided to call in at the Leprechaun to bring Laura up to date with his movements.

By now it was early evening although tonight the Leprechaun was unusually quiet. With the Melbourne Cup Carnival over, most of the racegoers were partied out and recovering at home.

'What'll it be, sir?' A girl he knew vaguely as Biddie stood waiting to take his order.

'Oh, I didn't come for a drink, I came to see Laura — er Em,' he corrected himself.

'Emily? Oh, she's gone — ' The girl looked around to see if anyone was listening and dropped her voice to a whisper. 'And under a cloud. Immigration.' She mouthed the word, rolling her eyes significantly. 'An' that's all I know.' She looked Declan up and down, deciding she liked what she saw. 'But I finish here at ten if you're looking for company — '

Her words fell on deaf ears; Declan was no longer listening. The worst of his predictions seemed to be coming true. Laura was in trouble and he needed to find her — now. After leaving the Leprechaun, he tried the girls' flat, ringing the doorbell several times and hammering on the door, receiving no answer. He stopped when another tenant opened their door a fraction to glare at him. The girls' flat had to be either empty or the occupants sound asleep.

Briefly, he called the Morgan stables and talked to the foreman who confirmed that Jodie had already arrived with Lancelot's Pride.

'He's a beautiful horse, Mr Martin,' the man enthused. 'Such a pity you have to sell him.'

Not wanting to continue this line of conversation, Declan asked to be transferred to the house and Foxie told him that her husband and Laura were still in town. From the tone of her voice, she didn't sound too happy about this news.

'And now, of course, she has to get back to Ireland before she's arrested,' Foxie complained. 'That girl is a magnet for trouble. She seems to go from one bad situation to another. If it isn't facing down armed bandits, it's hiding from Immigration — '

'Thank you, Foxie.' He cut short her torrent of criticism. Some women became placid and tolerant during pregnancy; clearly Foxie Morgan wasn't one of them. 'I'll maybe call Daniel in Kew.'

'It's a silent number — not in the book.'

'Then would you give it to me, please?'

Having extracted the number from Foxie, Declan decided to return to his motel before ringing them. He would need to make arrangements for his own departure as well as the sale of Lance. It was plain that he couldn't trespass on Daniel Morgan's generosity for too long. Foxie was already on the warpath.

Back at the motel, he was reminded only too vividly of the night he had spent with Laura although the sitting room was now tidy and his bed newly made with clean sheets and turned down. Also he checked his messages, seeing there had been a call from his uncle's home in Ireland. He groaned, wondering whether to return it at once or not. Although, with the time difference, it would still be breakfast time on that side of the world, Tavis was sure to be up and about, impatient for news about the sale of the horse. He decided to make the call rather than speculate; it was always better to know the worst.

In the event, it was Maureen and not his uncle who answered the phone, her voice thick with tears as if she had been weeping for some time.

'Oh Declan, thank God — my prayers have been answered. I'm so glad you called.'

'All right, Auntie Mo, I can tell you've been crying. What has the old devil done to upset you now?' It was something he had always detested — his uncle's bullying attitude towards his inoffensive and gentle aunt.

'Oh Declan, you wouldn't say such a thing if you knew. There's no easy way to tell you. Your Uncle Tavis is dead.'

'Dead? How?' Declan's mind whirled, considering all the possibilities. 'Was there an accident?' Certainly Tavis was well into his sixties but he had always seemed so strong, so full of life and vigour. It seemed impossible that he was so suddenly gone.

'The doctor has warned him for years about drinking too much but you know Tavis — never took any notice of anyone.'

'So what happened?'

'A massive stroke, so the doctor said. Followed by a heart attack. We didn't even have time to get him to hospital, he died before the ambulance got here. Oh Declan, I do wish you weren't so far away. How soon can you get back home?'

'I'll come at once. Soon as I can get on a plane,' Declan said softly, feeling guilty for not being more shocked and upset by his uncle's demise. Instead, he felt as if a weight of oppression had been lifted from his shoulders. It made him want to punch the air, shouting for joy. But for his Aunt Maureen's sake he had to conceal his true feelings. 'I shall bring Lance home, too. There's no need for us to sell him now.'

'I hope not, Declan, but I don't know.' His aunt's voice was low. 'Your uncle risked an enormous amount of money on Lance and he lost it. I'm not sure of our financial circumstances right now.'

'I kept telling him the competition was stiff but he was so sure Lance would win. I warned him to hedge his bets and back the horse each way.'

'Well,' Maureen laughed softly, 'You know he was never any good at taking advice.'

'But he was always so careful before — to the point of meanness.'

'I know. But these last months, he wasn't himself. He's always been hot-tempered but lately he would fly into a rage for no reason, especially when he had too much to drink. I was reaching a place where I almost detested him and I certainly hated the way he was treating you.'

'But you have the house and the stables. Surely he had the sense to leave them to you?'

'Perhaps. I'm not even sure that he left a will unless the lawyers have it.'

'Try not to worry too much. And remember, I have some Australian dollars for you — the money for Lancelot's third prize.'

'I really feel you should keep it. That money should be for you.'

'Let's wait and see, shall we? Have you arranged a funeral yet?'

'No. The coroner is involved as he died here at home. Declan, please, just get back here as soon as you can. I need you.'

'I will. And always remember, I love you, Auntie Mo.'

'Love you, too,' she said through her tears as she hung up.

★ ★ ★

Declan knew that as soon as he put down the phone, he should call the airline and make arrangements immediately for them all to go home, including the horse. Instead, he called Daniel's home in Kew. Aside from wanting, no almost longing, to speak to Laura, he knew he must tell his friend of his uncle's demise and the subsequent change of plans about the horse. His aunt had been less than optimistic about the state of his uncle's affairs but hopefully something could be salvaged and they would not need to sell Lance.

He tried ringing Laura's mobile but, as usual, she had neglected to charge it and calls to the house in Kew informed him that the line was engaged. He wouldn't take the chance of leaving a message. Finally, just as he was about to give up, the telephone was answered by Daniel with an impatient, 'Yes! Morgan here.'

'Daniel, it's Declan — I — '

'Sorry, mate, can it wait? I'm expecting an urgent call — '

'I'm sorry, too, Daniel, but it can't. My aunt in Ireland just called to say that my uncle has died and — '

'My God, Declan, that's awful news. I'm so sorry — sorry I was short with you, too. Were you close?'

'Not really. But I am worried about my aunt. It's been a shock and she's not taking it very well.'

'Is there anything I can do for you here?'

'Thanks but you've done more than enough already — accommodating Lance. Of course, I'll be taking him home now. Luckily, I didn't cancel his transport, hoping something would turn up.'

'But not something so drastic as this.'

'No.'

'Well, keep in touch and we'll fit in with your plans. But now, if there isn't anything else?'

'Oh but there is!' Declan sensed that Daniel was about to hang up. 'I understand

Laura's in trouble again and that she's with you?'

'And you'd like a word? Well, make it brief, would you? I'm calling in a few favours, waiting to hear when I can get her on a plane. With the Spring Carnival over, it seems that everyone wants to get out of Melbourne at the same time.'

'Thanks, Daniel — for everything,' Declan put in while he waited, hearing the phone change hands.

Then Laura's voice came on the line, breathy and a little uncertain.

'Declan? I — I was wondering when I would hear from you.'

'Sorry,' he said. 'I've had rather a lot on my mind.' Briefly, he brought her up to date with the news of his uncle's death, telling her that he would be leaving Australia himself as soon as he could confirm the transport for Jodie and Lance. At this moment, he sensed that she was almost holding her breath, waiting for him to make some sort of commitment — or even a promise to keep in touch when they were home. But the words stuck in his throat, remaining unsaid. It seemed that his uncle had left his Aunt Maureen nothing but trouble and he would have to deal with the lawyers on her behalf, untangling the mess Tavis Martin had made of his life. That could take some time. Only then could he give any thought to his own future and what it might hold. So the words he longed to say remained locked in his heart and he found himself making small talk instead.

'Have a pleasant journey, Laura. I'm sure we'll meet again before long.'

'Are you?' She came back at him, full of wounded pride. 'That's not very likely if I don't even have your address.'

'Don't you?' Almost reluctantly, he mumbled the phone number. 'Get in touch when you're settled.'

'Maybe I will and then maybe not.' Her voice was sharp with misery. 'After all, you live quite a long way from Dublin.'

'Laura, please. I can't deal with it now. Don't be like this.'

'Like what? I know how you felt about your uncle and I'm sure you're not grieving because he's dead.'

'Laura!' He heard Daniel's shocked tones in the background. 'Laura, don't — '

But she was determined to speak her mind. 'You're just as bad as Col Newbold. And that's hard because I really did think we had something, you and I.' She broke off, tears blocking her throat and making it impossible for her to speak.

'Well, there it is, isn't it?' he snapped back,

knowing the only way to end the hurt for both of them was to make it clean and quick. 'I'm sorry if you were misled. Be seeing you, Laura.'

'Not if I see you first,' she managed to get in before he hung up.

12

Declan let go a sigh of relief after seeing Jodie on to the plane to accompany Lancelot's Pride on his journey back to Ireland. Just as he feared, Foxie had taken a dislike to the little Irish strapper and he thought it prudent not to trespass on the Morgans' hospitality any longer. He had expected Jodie to be pleased to hear they were on their way home and was taken aback when she told him she wasn't.

'Why does it have to be now?' she moaned when he joined her in the Morgans' stables, advising her of his plans. 'Why can't we wait until after Christmas? Then Simon will be free to come with us. He has riding commitments until the end of this year.'

'I'm sorry but that can't be helped.' With his own romance on the rocks, Declan had little empathy for anyone else. 'If your relationship can't survive a separation for just a few months, then maybe it's not too solid, anyway.'

Jodie stared at him. It wasn't like Declan to be unkind but she could see he was in no mood to be softened by tears.

'All right,' she said at last. 'When do you want us to go?'

'Now. Fortunately, I never cancelled his booking. I want Lance to spend some time on his own turf and be ready for the next season at Ascot next year.'

'But that's ages away. And there's very good training here. Good fun, too. They walk horses on the beach and strengthen them by letting them swim in the sea. Lance would do just as well here until after Christmas. I'm sure Mr Morgan won't mind.'

'No, but Mrs Morgan *would*. From what she tells me, you haven't been getting along.'

'Been telling tales, has she?' Jodie's lips set in a sullen line. 'I don't know what she expected but I didn't come here to be her unpaid servant, I came to look after Lance.'

'All the same, you are a guest in her house. It wouldn't have hurt you to make yourself useful.'

'I did. But what a diva! Everything has to be just so for her.' Jodie was thoughtful for a moment. 'Some sort of actress, wasn't she? On TV?'

'Quite a famous one, I believe. But don't let her good looks fool you. She knows just as much about horses as you do.'

'I've yet to see it. No wonder Morgan

spends half his life in town.'

'You really don't like her, do you? That settles it. The sooner I can get you and Lance out of here the better.'

'Ohh, Declan!'

'No, Jodie, my mind is made up. We need to get back to Ireland as soon as we can. Maureen needs us. Whatever we might have thought, she loved that old man.'

'I know, I know.' Jodie's tone softened. 'The woman's a saint and I still find it hard to believe the old man is gone. Make the arrangements, Declan. I'll fit in with whatever you want.'

And now, having seen them on their way with Jodie more confident this time of handling the paperwork, he had only to get in touch with Daniel. His friend had insisted on taking his open return, offering to pull some strings to help him get back to Ireland fast. Declan leaped at the chance. Were it not for Daniel's intervention, he wouldn't have been able to get back to Ireland in less than three weeks.

Earlier that same day, when Laura hung up the phone on Declan and burst into noisy tears, Daniel had stared at her in amazement.

'What was all that about?' he said. 'Why did you speak to the poor bloke like that?'

'You've got it all wrong about Declan.' She spoke through a handful of tissues, muffling her speech. 'He isn't the person you think. He doesn't love me. Probably never did.' And she buried her face in the tissues, giving way to a fresh storm of tears.

'All right. What did he say to upset you?'

'Nothing. It's what he *didn't* say.'

'Laura, it's the telephone. Don't take it so much to heart. I've had more misunderstandings over the phone than any other means of human communication. Don't judge the man until you've had the chance to thrash it out, face to face.'

'Well, that isn't likely now, is it?' Laura wailed. 'We're going our separate ways and I'll never see him again.'

'Look, I can't hear myself think while you're making that noise. Go and find Mrs Wicks in the kitchen — get her to give you some ice cream or something.'

She scowled at him through her tears. 'Daniel, I'm not ten years old!'

'No? You could have fooled me.'

Just as Laura flounced off to the kitchen in search of tea and the comfort of cake, the telephone rang. It was Daniel's contact from the airline.

'I'm so sorry, Mr Morgan, I've done my best but there's not a seat to be had in

255

Economy for at least two weeks.'

'That could be awkward. What about standby?'

'Unreliable and already in overload.' The girl hesitated before going on. 'Look, I don't want to persuade you, but if it's really that urgent for your cousin to travel this week, I do have seats on a plane leaving for Singapore and London via Dubai in forty-eight hours — Business Class.'

'Business Class,' Daniel repeated, considering it. He had made an unexpected amount of money on Foxie's Fancy and had been thinking of surprising his wife with some diamond earrings. But it might be better to wait until the twins had safely arrived. And he hadn't yet given Laura a birthday present. 'OK, you're on,' He said cheerfully. 'It's only money, isn't it?'

'And, naturally, with your usual generous discount — '

'Thanks,' Daniel said as a radical idea popped into his mind. It would take a bit of planning and organization but he never backed away from a challenge. 'Let's confirm. You can get me a seat in Business Class in forty-eight hours? I don't suppose you could make that two?'

★   ★   ★

Declan checked in his small amount of luggage and received his boarding pass, surprised to find that Daniel had not only taken charge of arranging his transport but had come to see him off. Although they had common interests and had become firm friends during the few weeks they had known each other, he was surprised when Daniel offered to use his influence to get him back to Ireland in record time. And, rather than leave it for Declan to collect, he had turned up himself with the ticket in hand.

Once his luggage had been checked in and he was ready to move into the departure lounge, Daniel seemed fidgety and unusually anxious to be gone.

'I can't thank you enough,' Declan said. 'Without you, I know I wouldn't have been able to leave so soon.'

'Think nothing of it.' Daniel clapped him on the shoulder. 'If business continues to prosper, I've a fancy to come to Ireland again quite soon.'

'Well, I hope I'll be in a position to entertain you when you do.' Declan said, his smile faltering. 'I have no idea what I'll find when I get there.'

'You worry too much. Look at you. You have youth and talent on your side. What more can you possibly need?'

257

'A little of your optimism, perhaps.' Declan's smile returned. 'If I had only half of your drive and ambition, I'd be fine.'

'Look, I really do have to go,' Daniel said. 'Have a good flight and let me know as soon as you arrive.'

'Best wishes to Foxie and thank her for putting up with my awful girl.'

'Which one do you mean? Laura or Jodie?'

They parted, saluting each other and laughing.

★   ★   ★

Declan waited until the passengers were called for Economy. He hadn't flown with Emirates before and was looking forward to the change.

The girl at the desk frowned when she saw his ticket, saying he should have joined the passengers who boarded earlier, heading for Business Class.

'Not me. There has to be a mistake,' he said. 'I'm always in Economy — I never fly Business Class.'

'Well, you are this time. Someone must have arranged it as a surprise.' She smiled, passing him on to another girl who had come to escort him to his seat. 'Don't look so anxious — your ticket is valid and fully paid.'

Declan followed her, still feeling uncertain. His misgivings vanished when a pretty stewardess welcomed him aboard and he saw the comfortable window seat that had been reserved for him. Other seats filled with businessmen clutching briefcases and a grandmother travelling with her two young grandchildren. But still the seat beside him remained vacant and the stewardess started to glance at her watch, looking anxious.

At last he heard the door clang shut and, as he fastened his seat belt, the familiar irrational fear took hold of him. What good was a seat belt? It would only hold him in place while the plane crashed and burned. Closing his eyes, he groaned as the plane's engines roared into life and he sensed rather than saw someone hurriedly occupy the seat beside him. His hands felt cold as he clung to the armrests of his luxurious chair. If he were about to die, at least he would do it in style.

The plane slowly rolled towards the position on the runway from which it would leave and the pilot opened up all the engines to give them power enough to defy gravity and lift the big passenger craft off the ground. Every time he heard the plane vibrate in response, he felt sure they were never going to make it.

'Just let me get home in one piece.' He

murmured an anxious prayer as the plane increased speed until it was airborne, leaving the ground behind. 'An' I swear I'll never leave Ireland again.'

Hearing a familiar gurgle of laughter, his eyes snapped open and for a moment, he thought he was hallucinating. Laura was sitting in the seat beside him, laughing at his discomfiture.

'You can relax now,' she said. 'We're safely upstairs and I don't think we're going to crash.'

He stared at her for a moment, still finding it hard to believe she was there. Then they both said the same thing at once, still wary and mindful of the bad turn their last conversation had taken.

'What are *you* doing here?'

'We have Daniel to blame for this.' Laura was quick to identify the culprit. 'I thought he was acting strangely. Insisted on sending me home Business Class — said it was a belated birthday present. And then he kept me talking for so long, I almost missed the flight.'

Declan laughed shortly. 'An expensive way to play Cupid. He has us trapped here in each other's company for the next twenty-four hours, not knowing if we'll arrive the best of enemies or the best of friends.'

'I have never been your enemy, Declan,'

she said softly. 'Daniel made me see how childish, how thoughtless I had been. Whether you loved your uncle or not, you were still bereaved and I shouldn't have said what I did. But then you seemed so distant, so cold and I couldn't reach you. I felt as if you were closing the door on me. Pushing me away.'

Declan sighed. 'I didn't know what to say. I had so much I wanted to tell you — to ask you — but I didn't think it was fair. How could I ask you to marry me when I wasn't even sure I had a job?'

'Were you going to ask me, then?'

'I was thinking of it when Lance won third place. Until my uncle brought my world crashing about my ears.'

Laura felt her heart beginning to pound in anticipation. Maybe he did love her, after all. 'And if you had followed that plan and asked me, the answer would have been yes. Ohh, Declan —'

'Laura, slow down. We have to be practical here. I love you — of course I do — but I really don't know what I'll find when I get back to Ireland.'

'So what? You've more than proved yourself with Lancelot's Pride. You'll soon get another job if you need one.'

'That's what Daniel said.'

'And he's right.'

'Even if it means poverty and love in a rented cottage?'

'A lot of people start life together with less.'

Before he could reply to this argument, a blonde stewardess arrived, offering a tray of vintage champagne, sparkling enticingly in slender flutes.

'Oh yes, please.' Laura smiled up at her, already reaching out to take one.

'Laura, be careful,' Declan teased. 'I thought you said you were sworn off the drink for ever?'

'But this is champagne and we have to celebrate our engagement,' Laura whispered, handing the glass to him and accepting another for herself.

'Now hold on. I never said we were engaged.'

'Not yet, no. But it's only a matter of time. Think of Daniel. He'll be so disappointed if his matchmaking comes to nothing. Business Class is expensive.'

'Yes, I know, but — '

'You can buy me the ring when we get to Singapore — duty free.'

Declan lay back and groaned, closing his eyes. 'I don't think you've been listening to a word I've said.'

'No.' Laura's smile was complacent as she

sipped her champagne. 'And I'm not going to until you say something I want to hear.'

★ ★ ★

Singapore Airport was a maze of shops and bars to tempt the tourist into impulse purchases before resuming their journey. Laura and Declan found a jewellery shop where the assistant had smiled encouragement, making the assumption that this was an airline holiday romance. Declan was looking at sapphires but Laura thought they should settle for something more modest. While she was engrossed in looking at yet another tray of rings, the shop assistant took Declan to one side and leaned close, lowering his voice so that Laura shouldn't hear what he had to say. Declan recoiled from the powerful scent of his hair oil.

'Believe me, sir, you don't have to go to all this expense. There's no need to buy real gems for the young lady. We have a spectacular range of artificial diamonds set in rolled gold that only a jeweller could tell from the real thing.' He jerked his head towards Laura. 'And, if she happens to get it valued later, well, then . . . ' He shrugged. 'You'll be long gone.'

Declan went over to Laura, who was still

looking at diamonds with little enthusiasm. 'We're leaving right now,' He said, taking her arm. 'I don't want to buy anything here.'

She glanced up at him, unable to read his expression. There was no time to look in any more shops, it was time to rejoin their flight.

'I'm sure we'll find just the right thing in Dubai,' Declan said in answer to her querying look.

After a meal in flight and finding themselves exhausted after the drama of the past few days, they fell asleep holding hands and didn't wake until the plane began its early-morning descent to Dubai.

With Emirates everything seemed to happen so smoothly and they were momentarily stunned by the luxury that surrounded them in the Business Class lounge with its comfortable leather seats and panoramic windows overlooking the airport. After freshening up in the restroom and treating herself to some of the perfume on offer there, Laura made a bee-line for the internet facilities. She wanted to send an e-mail to Bridie, warning her that she was on her way home and that she would be in touch again before leaving Heathrow.

As their flight wouldn't leave until later that day, they now had plenty of time to browse through a number of duty-free shops full of things to entice them but somehow that special engagement ring continued to elude them.

Just as they were about to give up, they saw the very thing in the window of a small jeweller offering a range of restored and reset antique rings. It was a single large sapphire, surrounded by a ring of small emeralds and set in warm, antique gold.

'Emerald green,' Declan murmured. 'Of course. And with a sapphire to match your eyes. Would you like it?'

'I'd love it,' Laura said. 'But we have to be careful, Declan. I'm sure it's going to be too expensive.'

'I don't care,' he said. 'This ring will remind you of this journey that brought us together. We can worry about being careful when we get home.'

As soon as Laura put it on, she felt as if it already belonged to her. The ring fitted perfectly without any need for alteration and the style exactly suited her small hand.

'A Victorian piece,' the salesman commented. 'It's been sitting there waiting for someone with delicate hands.'

But when he named the price, Laura gasped and started to take it off, ready to return it.

'No, wait,' Declan said, addressing him again.

'What are we talking about here? You know that price is ridiculous and most women these days have much larger hands. You might wait a long time before it fits anyone else. No one's going to buy it if they can't try it on.'

'The size can be altered.' The man sighed, realizing that after all the sale wasn't going to be easy. 'We do it all the time.'

Laura could only wait with the ring on her finger, looking from one to the other like a spectator at a tennis match as Declan started the business of haggling with the owner of the little shop. His tenacity surprised her but ten minutes later the deal was closed with Declan handing over several traveller's cheques and refusing to let her see how many. Meanwhile, the jeweller continued to shake his head and grumble about cheap tourists who cheated him.

Outside, Laura studied the brilliant colours of dark green and blue on her finger, turning the stones to catch the light. 'You didn't really rob him, did you?' She glanced at Declan. 'It might bring bad luck.'

'Of course not.' Declan grinned. 'It's a tradition here. They never expect you to pay the first price they ask for.' He glanced at his watch. 'We'd better hurry now. We don't want to miss our flight and have our luggage arriving before we do.'

* ★ * ★ * ★ *

On this, the third leg of their journey, Declan was more relaxed as the plane left the runway and took to the air. Laura wanted the journey never to end. Up here above the clouds, they were in a world of their own. There was entertainment always on hand if they wanted it, although most of the time they preferred to chat, making plans for the future. They talked about everything, including their favourite foods and even the movies they liked or disliked. Laura didn't want to think of arriving in Dublin where they would be subject to outside influences and forced, for a while at least, to live apart.

'Don't look so sad,' he said as the plane touched down at Heathrow and taxied towards the terminal. 'This is just the beginning. I promise you, I won't let us be parted for long.'

'I don't know, Declan.' She stared out of the window, unaccountably depressed. Even from where they were sitting, they could see that autumn was giving way to a chilly, wet winter, the skies full of potential rain. 'Every time I come back it seems as if everything's changed.'

'And so it has.' Taking her left hand, he kissed the tips of her fingers and looked at the beautiful ring on her hand. 'You have my ring and my promise — even if it does turn out to be love in a cottage.'

She smiled at this, cheered by his confidence, as they left the plane and went out into the airport to face the lengthy business of going through Customs and arranging their ongoing flight to Dublin. Declan also telephoned his aunt and found out that Jodie was already home with Lancelot's Pride.

'Settled into his old quarters and none the worse for any of it.' Maureen seemed more cheerful and confident than when he had spoken to her last. 'And there's no holding Jodie — like a dog with two tails showing off her engagement ring to the other girls. They all want to go to Australia now.'

'And the funeral?' Declan said. 'I haven't missed it, have I?'

'It's on Friday morning. I left it as long as I could so that you would be home.' Only now did her voice sound a little less confident. 'And in the afternoon Tavis's lawyers are coming to read his will.'

'Well, there'll be no surprises there. He'll have left it all to you.'

'If there's anything left to leave,' she said softly.

'I'll be there soon, Auntie Mo. And I have

what I hope is a pleasant surprise for you, too.'

As they had arrived in London so late, they couldn't catch another flight until the following afternoon, so they took a taxi into town and booked into a small bed and breakfast hotel that Declan knew. It was run by an Irish woman who had strong views on the sanctity of marriage so she made sure their bedrooms were on different levels and opposite sides of her house.

'It isn't that I don't trust you,' she said, 'but it's no good putting temptation into your way. I remember what it was like to be young and in love.'

They exchanged a rueful smile. Worn out after their lengthy journey, all both of them needed was sleep in a comfortable bed; sex was the last thing on their minds. They both slept long and late until after 10 a.m. when the landlady came knocking, warning them that if they didn't get up and leave before midday, she would have to charge them for another night.

★　★　★

Dublin showed them no better weather than London, a steady downpour greeting their arrival. Declan spotted Laura's mother even before she did, recognizing an older, more substantial version of his bride-to-be. She swept Laura into an extravagant embrace and then stood back to look at her.

'My goodness, Laura, you're all grown up,' she pronounced. 'You went away a schoolgirl and came back a woman.'

'Mam, it's so good to see you,' she said, hugging her once again and registering the new lines of care on her mother's face. 'But I have someone I want you to meet. This is Declan Martin and we are — '

Bridie's eyes widened in pleasure, always ready to be impressed by a man's good looks.

'Mrs Winton.' Smiling, he took her hand.

'Oh please — I'll be free of that name soon as I can arrange it. Jus' call me Bridie like everyone else.' She gave him an oddly flirtatious glance from under her lashes before returning her attention to her daughter. 'Now you mustn't be cross with me. I promise it's only temporary but we're staying with Auntie Kit. I'm already back at the travel agency and I haven't had time to look for anything else.'

'Oh, no,' Laura groaned, unconsciously slumping against Declan. 'That's the worst news. I never imagined a home-coming like this.'

'Well, I can't help it.' Bridie shrugged. 'It is what it is.'

'Mrs — um — Bridie,' Declan put in. 'We haven't had time to tell you an' it's surely a bit late to ask for your blessing. But Laura and I are engaged — '

'Indeed you are not!' Bridie's happy expression turned quickly to one of suspicion and disapproval. 'How can you be? This is the first I've heard of it.'

'Well, it only just happened, didn't it?' Laura put in, showing Bridie her hand and the ring, sparkling on her finger.

'Well, you can just get unengaged until I know more about it,' Bridie demanded, her earlier good humour entirely gone. 'Who is this young man and where did you meet him?'

'He's a friend of Daniel and Foxie. And what's more, his horse, Lancelot's Pride, came third in the Melbourne Cup.'

'The Irish horse?'

'Yes.'

'So he's not an Australian then?'

'No, Mam. He's as Irish as Jameson's.'

'Then why the hell didn't you say so? Giving me a turn like that.' Bridie started to fan herself as a hot flush crept up from her throat and suffused her face. 'This always happens when I get overexcited — I come over all hot and bothered. I thought you were goin' to leave me all over again.'

'And so I am. I'm certainly not coming to live with old Auntie Kit.'

'You are so, too!' Bridie started to work herself into a temper again. 'Where else can you go where it doesn't cost board an' lodging?'

'Mrs — um — Bridie,' Declan broke in quickly before Laura's temper could rise to match her mother's. 'If I might make a suggestion. My aunt owns a racing stables jus' near Kilkenny where I'm going jus' now. It would be entirely proper and quite in order for Laura to stay there with my Aunt Maureen as a chaperon.'

'I don't know about that. And anyway, I haven't seen Laura for months.' Bridie wailed, sounding oddly like her daughter. 'She's only just home.'

It occurred to Laura that if her mother's relationship with Stanley Winton had prospered, Bridie wouldn't have cared if she'd never seen her again. But she bit her tongue and kept that thought to herself.

After a lot more persuasion from Declan, followed by the promise of a hearty meal before they left for Kilkenny, Bridie at last consented to let her daughter go.

'What a lovely man,' she confided to Laura while Declan went to hire a car. 'And with the gift of the blarney, too.'

* * *

Rather than visit a restaurant, Bridie suggested they have supper at a small pub near her Auntie Kit's home, where the food was known to be plain but good. They all did justice to a traditional Irish stew and everything seemed to be going well until after they'd eaten dessert and coffee was served.

Bridie sat up, toying with the spoon in her coffee. Knowing that gesture of old, Laura took a deep breath. Until now, Bridie had been content to make small talk, amusing them with her tales of Stanley Winton and his impossible relatives. But now it was as if the sun had retreated behind a cloud; Bridie's mood had changed.

'You do realize, Declan,' she addressed him, head on one side, 'that my daughter is still very young to be married — she is, after all, only eighteen.'

'Nineteen now, Mam,' Laura put in. 'It was my birthday just a few days ago — on Melbourne Cup Day this time.'

Caught on the wrong foot, Bridie had the grace to blush. With all that had been going on in her own life, she had quite forgotten her daughter's birthday. 'A few days hardly make a difference.' Her eyes glinted with temper. 'And I'll thank you not to interrupt when I'm

273

speaking. It isn't so long ago that twenty-one was the age for someone to marry without a parent's consent. And in my opinion that was no bad thing. It saved a lot of mistakes.'

'You made a big enough mistake with Stanley Winton.' The words fell out before Laura could stop them. 'And you're well past the age of asking permission from anyone.'

Bridie ignored the jibe. 'I am not the subject under discussion — you are, and Declan here. Now then.' She sat back, fixing him with her piercing gaze. 'If Laura's father were alive, he'd be asking what are your prospects? So I'll have to do it instead.'

'Well, as a matter of fact I — ' Declan cleared his throat and Laura broke in, realizing he was about to be much too honest.

'Oh stop it, Mam,' she said. 'We've just flown halfway round the world and we're both exhausted. Surely, this can keep for another time.'

'I don't think so,' Bridie said. 'Before he whisks you off to the depths of the countryside, I need to know what you're getting yourself into.'

'Not tonight.' Laura was firm, standing up and preparing to leave. 'We still have a two-hour drive ahead of us and it's getting late.'

'I agree with you. Tonight you can both

stay at Auntie Kit's. Declan will sleep on the couch, of course. Oh Laura, please. Poor old Kit will be so disappointed if you leave without seeing her.'

Laura didn't think so. Her great aunt had never looked on her with anything other than prune-faced disapproval. 'Anyway, she'll be in bed by now.'

'Then you can see her in the morning.'

Laura could think of nothing worse than waking up in Kit's claustrophobic little house and Declan deserved better than an uncomfortable night on that ancient two-seater couch with the springs poking through.

'No, Mam.' This time she was determined to win. 'We'll drop you off at the house and be on our way.'

Bridie opened her mouth, ready to argue, and closed it again. She didn't know how to deal with this new, decisive Laura, who refused to be cajoled or bullied by anyone.

Aware of all these undercurrents, they travelled the short distance to Kit's little house in silence. Laura sensed Bridie's relief when they saw the old lady had retired to bed, leaving the house in darkness. No welcoming light had been left for her, not even on the porch. Surreptitiously, Bridie popped a peppermint into her mouth in case Auntie Kit was about. She knew the old lady disapproved of wine.

Laura took her mother's hand before she got out of the car. 'It's no good for you, living here, Mam. You have to get away just as soon as you can.'

'You're right.' Suddenly, Bridie seemed close to tears. 'I was hoping it might be better, if you came to stay for a while — '

'It's not going to get any better.' Laura was firm. 'You need to find a nice little place of your own.'

'I will.' Bridie thought for a moment. 'There's a girl at work with a flat who needs someone to share an' since you're not going to be with me — '

'Then snap it up quick. Anything's better than living with Auntie Kit.' Laura gave her a rueful smile. 'Look, I won't be gone for ever. I'll call you at the travel agency.'

Bridie then said her goodbyes and even gave Declan a kiss. They watched her make her way to the front door and let herself in. She gave them a final wave without looking back.

13

Although Laura loved her mother and was happy that they were both back in Ireland where they would see each other more often, she was more than happy to be leaving her behind tonight. She settled back in her seat and breathed a deep sigh of relief. Her relationship with Declan was too precious, too new to stand up to such close scrutiny — and for now she wanted to keep it to herself. Bridie's attitude after dinner made her realize how far they had drifted apart and how unwilling she was to fall back into the old pattern of their relationship. *You went away a schoolgirl and came back a woman,* her mother said, making it sound almost like an accusation. And what did she really mean? That she could read her daughter's loss of innocence from the look in her eyes? Laura brooded, considering this, lost in thought.

'Penny for them,' Declan said when they had been travelling in silence for some time. 'You're unusually quiet. Are you OK?'

'Oh, I was jus' thinking of Mam an' how she's trying to take over, ruling my life as before,' she said, glancing across at him.

'Thanks for getting me off the hook. I couldn't bear to come all this way just to end up living with Auntie Kit.'

'Well, it wasn't entirely unselfish on my part. One way or another, I wasn't going to leave you behind.'

'And you never told her your uncle had died. I kept waiting for you to say something and you didn't.'

'I know and I feel bad about that.' Declan frowned, biting his lip. 'But she needed only the slightest excuse to keep you. If she had any idea there'd been a death in the family, she wouldn't have let you go.'

'No and now I'm thinking about the other end of the journey. Your Aunt Maureen. Is it fair to expect her to welcome a stranger at such a time? What if she doesn't like me?'

He glanced at her briefly. 'How not? She'll love you as I do and you won't be strangers for long. I'm all she has, you see. There are no other relatives apart from some distant cousin who took the veil. I'm sure she could do with the comfort of female company at this difficult time.'

'I hope you're right.' She glanced at the dashboard, seeing that it was after eleven. 'But isn't it rather late for us to turn up on her doorstep tonight?'

'I've already thought of that.' He took his

eyes from the road for a moment to smile at her, a wicked glint in his eye. 'I know of a nice little place not far from here. We can stay overnight and arrive rested and refreshed in the morning.'

Laura stiffened. 'Not somewhere you've stayed with other girls?'

His eyes widened although he kept them dutifully on the road. 'Great heavens, Laura, who do you think I am? Casanova? This is Ireland, remember? I had only one serious girlfriend before I met you.'

'That's all right, then.'

'Thank you.'

The slight atmosphere between them remained until he left the highway to take a bumpy side road which seemed to be used mainly by farm vehicles. At the end it widened into a circular driveway outside a picturesque farmhouse which had been converted into a small, private hotel. Although it was late, the front of the house was ablaze with lights with a sign offering vacancies in the front window as well as ample space for vehicles to park beside the front door.

'Stay here until we're signed in and I'll come back for you,' Declan said as he pulled up outside the front porch and got out of the car.

'What are you going to say? That we're newly married or you've got the harlot of Jerusalem out here?'

'Ssh!' Laughing, he put a finger to his lips. 'And I wish you'd stop making bad jokes.'

'I always do that when I'm nervous. Sorry.'

His smile faded and he leaned back into the car, trying to interpret her mood. 'Laura, if you don't want to do this, it's OK. I'll ask for separate rooms.'

'No, oh no!' She pulled him forward to give him a quick but bruising kiss on the lips. 'Of course I want to spend the night with you. After the plane journey and that last night in London, we've been apart quite long enough.'

'Don't worry — we'll be apart again. My aunt is old-fashioned, too.'

'Then let's not waste any more time tonight. Get inside and lay claim to our room.'

★   ★   ★

Laura didn't know what Declan had said to the landlady but she led them upstairs to what she called her honeymoon suite: an attic bedroom which was spacious enough although the ceiling was low. The king-sized bed was made all the more inviting, covered with a beautiful, handmade patchwork quilt in jewel colours with pillows to match. The mood of romance was carried through with Renaissance prints of medieval knights and their ladies on all the walls. The whole house was warmed with efficient central heating and there was a bathroom adjoining for their use alone. When the landlady left, smiling like a conspirator to retreat to the floors below, Laura turned to Declan.

'What did you say to her?' she whispered, although the woman was well out of earshot.

'Only that we haven't had time to have a honeymoon yet,' he murmured, drawing her into his embrace. 'It isn't quite a lie.'

Declan occupied the bathroom first, wanting to shower and shave and promising to run a bath for her when he'd finished. Meanwhile she unpacked her toiletries, wishing she had prettier nightgowns that didn't resemble oversized T-shirts. Luckily, she did have the antique kimono Foxie had given her for her birthday and hadn't yet worn. With the traditional wide sleeves, it was made of the softest pure silk and in dramatic shades of scarlet and black. It suited her colouring, Foxie said.

Returning from the bathroom naked except for his boxer shorts, his dark hair flattened because it was still wet, Declan's eyes widened at the sight of her in that kimono.

He smelled of a lemony cologne or aftershave and Laura tried not to stare at his muscular shoulders and slender torso, still bronzed from the Australian sun. Until now, she had never realized he had such good legs, the calves long and shapely, the thighs firm. Her stomach lurched in anticipation of what was to come; it felt as if it were full of butterflies, fluttering madly to get out.

'Go and get your bath,' he ordered, shooing her in the direction of the bathroom. 'And don't take too long. Give me a yell if you want me to come and scrub your back.'

She gave a small shriek of mock fright and ran to the bathroom. She bathed more quickly than she had intended, afraid he might have fallen asleep before she returned.

Feeling refreshed and invigorated after her bath, she came back to find he had switched off all the lights except a dim one beside the bed. He was lying on his back on top of the bed, ankles crossed and hands linked behind his head. While waiting for her, he had put on the TV and was watching a cricket match taking place somewhere hot as the sun blazed over the scene. He switched it off at once, making the room seem oddly silent after the noisy cheers of the crowd.

'Leave it on if you're watching it,' she said. 'I don't mind.'

He smiled back at her, knowing very well that she did. 'I didn't set all this up to lie in bed and watch cricket,' he said. 'I came here to lavish attention on you.' And he was off the bed in an instant, drawing her into his embrace and pulling her down towards him, making her catch her breath in surprise. He held her close as if she were infinitely precious, breathing in the scent of her newly washed and dried hair — she always used the same expensive shampoo as it made her hair smell of freshly picked apples. It was one of her few extravagances.

'You're so perfect, so lovely,' he said, gazing into those eyes that seemed to him dark as the deepest parts of the ocean, the pupils wide. 'I have to be the luckiest man in the world.'

Their kiss was long and satisfying and it was some moments before they could break apart, both needing air.

Laura wouldn't confess it but she was nervous, having only hazy and disjointed memories of the first time they had made love. The only thing she remembered was that it hurt initially and she was tense in case it did so again. Intuitively, Declan sensed this and was patient with her quivering nervousness, not undressing her until she was relaxed and ready and soothing her with undemanding kisses and long, languid strokes of her body. Only when she sighed and turned towards him with a dreamy look in her eyes, silently showing him she was ready, did he turn to the bedside table. He didn't mean to be unprepared for this second encounter. She leaned over, staying his hand.

'I wouldn't mind if we started a baby,' she whispered. 'It seems so calculating to — '

'No, Laura, not yet,' he whispered back, kissing her ear. 'I don't know how my uncle has left things at Kilkenny. Maureen might even have to sell up and I could be out of a job.'

'So what? It makes no difference to me. Whatever happens, I'm not going to lose you,' she said, burying her face in his neck and kissing the hollow of his throat. 'We're here together tonight and that's all that matters to me right now.'

They made love more than once, Laura's confidence increasing as their bodies became attuned to each other's needs. Consequently, they didn't sleep until the early hours and didn't wake until the landlady came knocking, bringing an enormous breakfast on a tray. Laura slid down in the bed, not wanting the woman to see she was naked.

'People who don't get enough sleep need to keep up their strength with good food.' The landlady winked at Declan. 'I know how it is with newly-weds.'

Laura gave Declan a jab in the ribs with her elbow but he ignored it, sitting up in bed to accept the tray. There was a full, cooked breakfast for both of them, including freshly brewed coffee, with toast and home-made marmalade to follow.

'Enjoy!' the woman said, heading for the door where she paused. 'Oh and take your time leaving — there's no need to rush. I have no one else booked into the honeymoon suite for tonight.'

'Declan!' Laura whispered when she was sure the woman was out of earshot. 'She'd have a pink fit if she knew we weren't married.'

'Well, she'll find out eventually.' Declan sat casually, as he attacked his breakfast with gusto. 'I forgot until I saw her that she's one of Maureen's best friends. Luckily, she doesn't remember me — yet.'

'Declan! I hope you didn't give her your real name? She'd know at once.'

'Hardly. Martin isn't such an unusual name. But no. I told her we were a Mr and Mrs Flanagan instead.'

Laura giggled. 'Well, I hope she doesn't know *my* mother, that's all.'

* * *

Unable to get enough of each other, they didn't resume their journey until almost midday, not arriving at the Martin Racing Stables until well after one.

'You never told me it was so beautiful,' Laura said as they drove through the paddocks and past a row of granite stables with shining wooden doors.

Declan sighed with contentment. Until he saw it again, he didn't realize how much he had missed the old place. It was good to be home. 'It looks even better in spring and summer,' he said. 'Aunt Maureen has hanging baskets of flowers all along the length of it.'

'Look, there's Jodie.' Laura leaned out of the window to wave to the red-haired girl, who came up to speak to them, hands on hips.

'You took your time getting here.' She gave them a knowing look. 'Better get on up to the house. Mrs Martin has been frettin', waiting on you.'

It struck Laura that the sprawling farmhouse that stood alongside the stables was gloomy and old-fashioned, perhaps reflecting the sorrow of the woman who waited for them within. But, once inside, that image was quickly dispelled. Certainly, the entrance hall was decorated with heavy-framed pictures of champion horses from an earlier era but the sitting room beyond was warm and welcoming with a log fire blazing in the grate and decorated in rich shades of dark red and ochre. Antique paisley shawls were flung casually over the back of a comfortable old-fashioned couch.

Declan's Aunt Maureen was also a surprise. Laura had been expecting a rather frail, white-haired elderly lady, dressed in sensible, old-fashioned tweeds or black. She couldn't have been more wrong. Maureen Martin was a vigorous woman in perhaps her late fifties, wearing clothes that were unmistakably new and in the half-mourning colours of pale mauve and lavender — colours she knew would suit her much better than unrelenting black. She wore boots, yes, but with high heels, not the heavy lace-ups old Irish women once loved to wear. Her make-up was subtle but flattering and her shoulder-length hair had recently been styled and streaked with gold. She looked almost glamorous.

Declan hurried to embrace her while Laura gave him a *why didn't you tell me?* look from behind his aunt's back.

'Auntie Mo,' he said. 'If I didn't know you better, I'd say you were wearing perfume.'

'I am, too. Do you like it? I took myself to

Dublin and had a makeover. It made me feel like a new woman — much better now.' Realizing that Declan wasn't alone, she turned, ready to greet Laura. 'But we're being very rude. Aren't you going to introduce me to this young lady who's staring at me as if I'm not at all what she expected?'

'Oh, I'm sorry,' Declan pulled Laura into their circle. 'Auntie Mo, this is Laura — Laura Flanagan. I met her on the plane on the way to Australia and we're — '

'Pleased to meet you, I'm sure.' Maureen held out a hand in polite welcome, somehow indicating that she wasn't.

'An' I'm very pleased to meet you, Mrs Martin.' Laura found herself gushing to cover the awkward moment. 'Declan has told me so much — so many nice things about you.'

'Ah!' Maureen's posture relaxed. 'Not from Australia then?'

Laura and Declan exchanged a smile, having been through all this with Bridie before.

'No, Auntie Mo. She's from Dublin and Irish as you are.'

'Well, you can't blame me for being concerned.' Maureen gave Laura a brief but genuine hug. 'I thought she was about to whisk you away again to the other side of the world.'

From that moment on, Declan felt almost superfluous as Laura bonded with Maureen, who wanted to know every detail of how they had met. Satisfied that they would chatter for hours, Declan took the opportunity to visit the stables and check up on Lance as well as catch up on the latest news from the stable foreman, John O'Shea.

'He seems to have taken no harm from the journey,' he said to John as the big gelding came to the door of his stall to greet him, snuffling and nibbling the collar of his coat, hoping for a treat. 'He looks well.'

'So do you.' The stable foreman greeted him with a handshake and a slap on the back. 'Get plenty of sun over there?'

Declan smiled, ignoring the question and going straight to what he needed to know.

'How are things here, John? Really?'

The older man sighed. 'Not as bad as they could be and at the same time not as good. One or two owners took horses away when your uncle died and I had to lay off two of the casual hands. Jodie's full of herself, of course, now that she's engaged. We're a bit like a ship without a rudder at the moment. I do my best but your uncle had his own way of doing things and never liked taking advice. What we really need' — he looked speculatively at Declan — 'is someone with modern ideas to take charge and give the old place a shake.' He looked hopeful. 'Maybe after they've read his will — '

'Don't look at me, John.' Declan smiled ruefully. 'I've no idea why because I spent my whole life trying to live up to his expectations but Tavis always disliked me. I'm not expecting anything but a kick in the pants from his will.'

★ ★ ★

It rained on the day of Tavis Martin's funeral, the sea of black umbrellas at the graveside adding to the gloom. Laura shared one with Declan, huddling close, chilled by the grim winter weather, while Maureen stood under another, aloof from everyone else, dry-eyed and strangely composed. Declan watched her uneasily; it wasn't like Maureen, whose emotions were usually very much nearer the surface. Laura's mother was also there, having subjected her daughter to a barrage of questions, demanding to know why the news of this death had been kept from her.

'Because I knew this would happen.' Laura had retorted. 'I don't know how but you manage to make a drama out of everything.' She changed the subject, hoping to deflect her mother from continuing this line of discussion. 'Have you moved into that flat yet with the girl from work?'

'No and I don't need to now.' Her mother's smile was smug. 'You're not the only one capable of getting engaged.' And she waved an enormous diamond under her daughter's nose. 'I'm marrying Mr Sampson when my divorce from Stanley comes through.'

'Old Mr Sampson? From the travel agency?' Laura could scarcely believe her ears.

'He isn't so old.' Her mother sniffed at the criticism.

'You don't even know his first name.'

'I do. It's Clement.'

'But you always said you didn't like him and what an old woman he was.'

'Well, I was mistaken, wasn't I? He's a very sweet man.'

'A very rich man,' Laura muttered, thinking of the recent takeover of two other agencies.

'He said it was only after I'd gone that he realized how much he missed me.'

'Wait a minute. He's a staunch Catholic, isn't he? He'll never marry a woman who's been divorced.'

'That's all you know. He says that as Stanley's an American an' we didn't get married in church, it doesn't count.'

Laura had shaken her head, speechless. And now she looked across at her mother, dressed in another new suit and expensive black felt hat, wondering if she had ever understood her at all.

* * *

The rain stopped as soon as the funeral was over and Maureen stood to one side, bracing herself for the onslaught of mourners who would descend on her home with expectations of good food and drink. She smiled briefly at everyone who came up to offer condolences, still dry-eyed and very much in control of herself.

'Are you all right?' Laura slid an arm around Maureen's waist when they arrived home, only moments ahead of the convoy of cars that was following them. 'If you're not feeling up to it, I can play hostess and feed the mob. You can go to your room.'

'Thank you, Laura, but I'm fine,' Maureen said. 'Don't fuss.'

'Sorry but I'm worried about you — so's Declan.'

'Then tell him to stop.'

* * *

It was after two when the last visitor, Laura's mother, had been persuaded to leave and Mr Gateshead, Tavis's solicitor, joined them in the sitting room and opened his briefcase, preparing to read the will. He had asked for Maureen, Declan, John O'Shea and Jodie Carpenter to be present. Laura sat with Declan, holding his hand; he was clearly anxious, wondering what his uncle might have to say about him. Jodie was the only one who seemed overcome by any emotion at this time, sniffling into a wad of tissues.

'Er — yes.' Mr Gateshead adjusted his spectacles before launching into it. 'This seems to be a pretty straightforward will so I'll waste no more time in reading it. *This is the last will and testament*, hmm — hmm I'll read out the smaller legacies first.'

'*To John O'Shea who has been my excellent stable foreman for many years and who has never been told how valuable an asset he is, I leave twenty thousand euros. I wish I could be there to see his surprise. To Jodie Carpenter, one of the best strappers in the business, I leave ten thousand euros. The poor girl is so plain, I'm certain she'll never marry, so I leave her this token amount towards the comfort of her old age.*'

Here, Jodie gasped, giggling and clapping a hand to her mouth. 'Do I still inherit if I get married?' she asked the solicitor, who held up a hand for silence.

'Questions afterwards.' he said. 'I'll proceed.'

'*I have thought long and hard about the disposition of my estate but finally I have reached the conclusion that blood is indeed thicker than water. It isn't my nephew's fault that in looks he resembles my feckless, younger brother. Therefore I bequeath my property, my own horses and all my investments — with the exception of the small legacies mentioned above — to my nephew, Declan Martin, and my wife Maureen Martin, to be shared equally between them.*'

'Signed and witnessed, etc, etc,' Mr Gateshead concluded. 'Clear cut and perfectly legal and valid.'

For the first time that day, Maureen burst into tears and Jodie leaped from her seat to capture Mr Gateshead, to make quite sure she wouldn't lose the money if she married Simon. Declan sat in stunned silence until John O'Shea came up to shake him by the hand and congratulate him, wishing him all the best.

'So,' he said, 'it seems as if we're going to get that shake-up and a few modern ideas about the place after all.'

When Mr Gateshead finally left, after consuming large quantities of tea and Maureen's home-made cake, John and Jodie left to relay the news of their good fortune to their respective partners, leaving the Martins and Laura alone. The room seemed oddly quiet with everyone gone.

'Thank the Good Lord your uncle came to his senses,' Maureen said at last. 'Ever since you came into this house, he resented it. I tried to reason with him, telling him how wrong it was to take out his sorrow and bitterness on a blameless child.'

'Why was that, Maureen? I never understood.'

She sighed. 'It was all so long ago. But he never forgave his younger brother for stealing and marrying the girl he wanted for himself.'

'My mother. Your sister. Do you know, I can scarcely remember her.'

'They were the beautiful ones — Kieron and Meryl. Tavis's younger brother and my little sister. It was Tavis who brought her to this house but as soon as she saw Kieron, my sister had eyes for nobody else. Tavis was so long forgotten, he might not have existed for her. So, when he asked me to marry him, I knew all along it was only to keep Meryl close

— he was never in love with me.'

'So, why?' Laura said. 'If you knew that, why did you marry him?'

'How young you still are.' Maureen smiled at her. 'Everything has to be perfect, doesn't it? So ideal. It's different now but in those days a single woman was looked upon with something akin to pity. Unless, of course, she chose to become a bride of Christ. I preferred a more secular life. As Tavis's wife, I could have my own home with the status attached to that position. It was what I wanted from life.'

'But why did he take such a dislike to Declan?' Laura persisted. 'When the woman he loved so much was killed in that accident, you'd think he would welcome her child.'

'I haven't told Declan this before and maybe I shouldn't now.' Maureen hesitated for a moment before going on. 'But it wasn't an accident.'

'Not an accident?' Declan said. She had all his attention now.

'Meryl had been told she was dying and had only a few weeks to live. Kieron didn't want to go on without her — so — they decided to cheat fate by going together.'

'A suicide pact. Are you telling me he deliberately drove into the path of that train?'

'I'm so sorry.' Maureen took a deep breath.

'I knew Meryl was sick and she made me promise that if the worst happened, I'd take you and raise you as my own. Of course, I agreed. I knew how ill she was but I had no idea what they meant to do. And afterwards, after the — the accident, Tavis went raving mad in his grief. He said crazy things — that their souls would be damned for ever and his brother had condemned them both to eternal hell. I had to keep you out of his sight for days, waiting for him to calm down. And that's it. The rest you know.'

Declan knew that for Maureen this was a long speech. Saying nothing, he put his arms about her, allowing her to give way to her emotions at last and cry on his shoulder.

'It's all right,' he said at last. 'I didn't lose anything. No one could have been a better mother than you, Auntie Mo.'

★ ★ ★

Although they offered to wait, out of respect for Tavis, Maureen saw no reason why Laura and Declan shouldn't get married right away. Bridie, full of her own plans to marry her elderly groom in the spring, made few objections herself, the only stumbling block being Laura's choice of wedding dress.

297

'What a pity I don't still have mine,' Bridie said.

'Oh, no. Not that eighties thing with the wide shoulders and ropes of pearls? Good grief, Mam, you'd have me looking like Joan Collins.'

'It was a beautiful gown and very expensive. I wish I had it now.'

'No, you don't. It was very much a fashion of its time. Nobody wears eighties clothes any more — unless they're going to a costume party.'

'Then what will you do? It's nearly Christmas, you know. There isn't time to have anything specially made.'

'I don't need to. What about your mother's dress with the lace skirt that went on for ever and little seed pearls on the bodice?'

'You can't be thinking of wearing that old thing?' Bridie wrinkled her nose. 'It's probably disintegrated by now with the lace gone in holes. I don't even know where it is.'

'I do. It's wrapped up in tissue paper in Auntie Kit's camphor trunk.'

'That's it, then. She doesn't like anyone poking about in there.'

Laura smiled wickedly. 'What she don't know won't hurt her.'

The wedding ceremony was small and intimate with only close family invited to attend. Declan asked John O'Shea to be his best man and, seeing the older man's face light up with surprise and pleasure as he did so, he knew he had done the right thing. And when Laura saw Declan's expression as she walked slowly towards him on Clement Sampson's arm, past the smiling faces of her family and close friends, she knew she was doing the right thing, too. Only Auntie Kit seemed to disapprove, giving Bridie a sharp jab with her elbow and making her wince.

'Where did she get that dress?' the old woman demanded in a stage whisper. 'If I didn't know better, I'd say it was the one my sister wore. I thought the neckline was disgracefully low then — '

'Hush, Auntie Kit.' Bridie tried to stem the old lady's flow of words. 'The service is about to begin.'

Laura's memory of her wedding was hazy. She felt as if she were seeing the world through rose-coloured spectacles, her feet scarcely touching the ground. Vaguely, she was aware of the priest and his warning about the solemnity of these vows but she couldn't stop smiling. And when Declan placed the plain golden band on her finger — somehow he had managed to find one exactly the same rose-gold as her engagement ring — her happiness was complete. Films and photographs were taken and still she smiled.

The reception, given by Maureen at their home, was also small and only for close family and friends. Jodie was excited as Simon was there, having promised to come to Ireland in time for Christmas. He had asked her to contact an agent who had agreed to find him work in the New Year. He brought good wishes and gifts from Daniel and Foxie as well as Daniel's promise to visit them in Ireland soon after the twins were born.

At last the champagne was finished, the food had been eaten and the wedding cake had been cut. All that remained was for the couple to leave.

'But where are we going?' Laura was mystified. 'You said you were needed here and couldn't afford to leave the stables right now. You said — '

'Oh, I know.' He gave her a quick kiss to silence her. 'But I think we deserve just a couple of nights, don't you? After all, it's business as usual on Monday.'

'But where?'

She didn't have to wait long to find out. Their car had received a wedding day make-over from Jodie. Garish balloons with painted faces and hearts strained to break free of the roof rack and tin cans rattled behind but Declan wouldn't stop to remove any of it. In less than half an hour they were leaving the road to take a bumpy track that Laura was quick to recognize.

Hearing their noisy arrival, the landlady came out to greet them, arms folded and with an expression of mock severity on her face.

'Well, well,' she said. 'Here for your second honeymoon, are you?'

Other titles published by
The House of Ulverscroft:

STARSHINE BLUE

Heather Graves

Jimmy Flynn has devoted his life to the champion Starshine Blue, after rescuing him as a foal from a burning stable. Hiding the fact that he is really James Kirkwood Jr., son of a hotel magnate, he has no wish to be drawn into his father's business empire. Even after winning the heart of Leila Christensen, his boss's daughter, he keeps his true identity from her. But Leila does not like to be deceived and their fragile happiness is threatened when unexpected events force Jimmy's secret into the open and he must face up to the future his father planned.

RED FOR DANGER

Heather Graves

Leaving behind a career in an American soap opera, Foxie Marlowe returns to Melbourne to comfort her recently widowed mother and take over her father's racing stables. However, she learns that during her father's illness, Daniel Morgan — the son of a family friend and the man with whom she once had an affair — rescued the business. Foxie believes that Daniel has taken advantage and stolen her inheritance, until he convinces her to join him as a business partner. Ignoring her lawyer's advice, she invests both her money and emotions in Daniel. But can she really trust him?

FLYING COLOURS

Heather Graves

With a broken romance behind her and a promising future ahead Corey O'Brien intends to concentrate on her chosen career. She certainly doesn't expect to come to the attention of someone like Mario Antonello, a racehorse owner and heir to a fashion house . . . Their first meeting isn't friendly so she is surprised by the interest he shows in her later. It all seems too much and it will take a while for Corey to find out the truth. Then she discovers a shocking secret and feels she must turn her back on him forever.

THE SNOWING AND GREENING OF THOMAS PASSMORE

Paul Burman

Something strange has happened to Thomas Passmore. Waking from a warm Australian beach, he finds himself at Heathrow Airport on a winter's morning, only he can't remember getting there. Burdened with emotional baggage and a sense of deja vu, Thomas pieces together fragments of his life by walking through the shadows of his past. Haunted by his father's suicide, his mother's rejection and by memories of his first love, his increasingly bizarre journey takes him into a world where one man's struggle to live again, as timeless as the battle of the seasons, becomes a choice between loss and life.